AH WELL

and

AND
TO YOU
ALSO

AH WELL

A Romance in Perpetuity

and

AND
TO YOU
ALSO

Jack B. Yeats

Routledge & Kegan Paul
London

Ah Well *first published in 1942*
by George Routledge & Sons Ltd
© *Copyright Michael and Anne Yeats 1942*
And To You Also *first published in 1944*
by George Routledge & Sons Ltd
© *Copyright Michael and Anne Yeats 1944*
Reprinted in one volume in 1974
by Routledge & Kegan Paul Ltd
Broadway House, 68-74 Carter Lane
London EC4V 5EL
Printed in Great Britain by
Lowe & Brydone (Printers) Ltd, Thetford, Norfolk

ISBN 0 7100 7665 7 (c)
ISBN 0 7100 7666 5 (p)

I wish to thank the Editor of the *Bell* for
permission to reprint two extracts and the
drawing of 'The Secluded Town' in *Ah Well*

CONTENTS

IT WAS A VERY SECLUDED TOWN

AH WELL

A Romance in Perpetuity

'DEATH where is Thy Sting?' We can all say that with cheerful courage every now and then. But who can say it always, who can say it always for a little rabbit lately fallen in death lying in a woodland path in the folly of immobility? This is everything—this flat world is everything. It is flat to us all. Though reason can give us a globe all printed with countries and varnished to hold in our soft round hands. But it is flat to us on the land. We can walk on it, and on the sea our ships can furrow about. There are solid waves on the land and shifting waves on the sea, but still it is all as flat to us as a carpet. But away from thoughted flatness there is a way of space, so we may call it, where there are no things. When we see a waterfall rushing up into the sky to lick a star, we don't want to say: What sort of a thing is that? We just want to cut a little slit and let 'thing' drop out of our vocabulary. If we drop a word which we don't care much about every little while we might find ourselves understanding the boys who disintegrate space so as to make a little nest for themselves in which to live and take the polish off their ideas.

It would be amusing to be using words for the last time. Careless or careful, letting them float away like paper money of an inflated coinage. While any man makes a picture in his mild memory to match with a word, 'Coinage' makes him see round metal discs, and inflating them gives him the laugh.

I knew a tiny boy, five years of age, I had heard loving proud parents repeat the wisest prantlings of their bantling. But I do not believe he said: "That's an awful girl that Nanna. She's hid the Aspirin again and I want to sit down and write my blasted old autobiography".

Yes, behind a curtain they play out their games, those others, in a fair land where fashion never becomes quaint. "Doctor, you like it here?" "Yes, no one knows whether I'm a doctor of divinity, medicine or law."

"The conversation is good?"

"Yes, splendid. Anyone speaks as he likes and answers himself. The ladies like it. There are some splendid ones here. Quite the old style and yet new up-to-date." And as he spoke to me, they passed like a whirlwind, and then more slowly they drifted over him like a mist of daisies hiding a field.

"How do you spend your years?" I said to one grand shining fellow.

"We spend them in having good thoughts of you and yours."

And then the curtain so dark, stiff and heavy fell down again from above bristling to the floor. And I saw a small boy, seven or eight years of age, his clothes worn out and tattered, but his face gay and glistening. I saw him on the limb of a tree. He had in his hand a small egg, it was warm. He was robbing a wild bird's nest. He heard the bird give a tearful cry. I saw him put back the egg gently with his

4

stubby fingers and he slid to the ground. He went a few paces from the tree and he turned his head and saw the bird rustling back to her eggs, and his face was dyed a purple black with the sudden flow of his wild childhood. But may be that boy is dead long ago. I can imagine other boys. I can imagine I am sitting on an old chair and I have before me a curtained screen and on my hands I have puppets, Punch boy and Judy girl, and I can push my hands through the curtain and up over the top of the screen, and I can talk for those two, and I can imagine behind them a great arc of indigo, smeary and distant, everlasting, never fading. But I must fade for I will get tired of imagining.

But my oldest friend, my unshatterable friend of clay. He is a dusty brown. He is the small man come away from his setting. He is the man just seen when

Once on a day
When days were good
In a day of long ago
When an old brown man
On a small brown horse
Rode up a whingey hill
And stood against a sinking sun—
That sun is sinking still.

He sits on my table, just brushing away what he finds there to make room for himself. He dangles one leg in the easy style. He wears his hat because indoor and out of doors are all the same to him.

5

And he would like perhaps to play that old game of 'I remember' or 'Don't you remember?'.

Don't you remember
Sweet Alice Benbolt.

He doesn't remember her. He's cute enough to pump up a memory from nowhere that would satisfy most people but not me. Where the old man ought to have a heart he has a hollow place and in it a hollow bell without a clapper. That hollow place for a heart—that empty bell is the widest possession he has, for he is a spare man. His bones rustle when he moves, but they are good bones close in the grain and tough. None of them has ever snapped, though he gave them many chances. Now he talks to me :

Now you are a man grown put away those childish things, let us talk about, or let us think about, the only subject fit for the children of a sovereign race. Let us think about Romance—R o o o o mance. That's the way they troll it out on the films, and so they should for if it hadn't been for an Irish Jew, called Bret Harte, wistful and envied in the mornings, looking on the coast of Sanfrancisco for comfort and making it for himself with Romance, there would be no film industry. But Romance is always to be found, not under the stones where the little crawly things are, but flowing in the hot breezes on the hot hillsides. There's sweat in Romance. If when the whanging stomached Irish who fled to America

6

after the famine had been listened to as valuers of John Bull, instead of listening to the little John Bull's valuing of the Irish, it was just a toss up, there would have been no sententious Abraham Lincoln to father his country. No war of the North and South. And what a magnificent Nation the American Nation might have been just now. Still there's bones in the soup and even bales of hay can be worked through. There's always another side—every morass has two sides. The one you step off into it, and the one to step on out of it, but still there it is. And it's only a question of time, and we the good fellows, all hope there's still enough of it left. Where there is Romance left there is 'the make up' I was going to say, but make up has another meaning more readily taken. A surface make-up on a face. Where there is Romance there is the grain, the seed of the charlock bui the wild gold weed of a free sovereign people growing. It was in Mother Eve's Garden and when the snake came sliding he circled it. He knew his match, my friend, juvenile friend.

What are you talking about 'Juvenile'? Look to yourself old Elfin Locks, I say, and that old brown friend pretends not to hear me. He stands by my easel now. Out of respect to it he takes off his hat and puts it down on my paint box, which is the top of a chest of three drawers. And the hat touches my palette, and I take it up, and look at the under-side of its brim, and just as I thought, there are flecks and smears of green paint and dabs of crimson, lip stick colour. I show them to old Brown and he is fascinated to

7

think that any lips should kiss his hat brim. He's in great form, he's in cackling form for a moment. But I must get a clean white rag and turpentine and clean up his hat brim. He likes the smell of turpentine. He drank a short drink once, a drink brought from far, from fir tree tops. It tasted like the smell of turpentine. But O, but it was good, so dry, so cheering, so like a fair dawn, he says now:

I have an old acquaintance. Oh, very old, he's lived a life of excitements of the body and the spirit. I would say his health had been a long shaking for the last forty years of it. Staggering away to wars, never fit, always with a stripped stern riding on a hard new saddle, and he says he would now live all his life over again in exactly the same way as the first time, doing the same things, having the same troubles for the same satisfactions. He believes it. Though I think six months of a warmed oven hash would drive him into the ground scraping out his grave of retirement with his own paws and no manicure. I myself would live short spells again. There are ten dawns I would see again—if I was able. If I could describe them so as to make them come back in memory to myself I could paint them, myself—me, who know no more of painting than my old hat did. Nevertheless, the one thing would bring the other, that I know. If I could remember I could colour my memory on that clean canvas with its face to the wall there in the corner. It waits my inspiration and still waits. Robert Louis Stevenson knew about the dawn but he swallowed it. My

8

dawns are my own unsucked, unswallowed lollipops of child's delight. They float before my eyes, but they are on a tide that moves too swiftly for me to measure their finery. Every man has his particular finger prints, and finger prints are a poor entertainment against a dawn.

Dawn is for the men. Sunsets for the ladies. Men all for hope, the women for musings, they say. As a matter not for arguments, it's the other way about. These things ought to be, as is always the way with those two, man and woman, here as I draw it out, in a Round Robin. And he scrawled with a stub of pencil on my palette the word 'woman' in a circle joining the end of n to the beginning of w.

I didn't know you could draw.

I can do everything. But still Hope and Musing aren't so far out. Man always hopes to be brave, manly and all that, and woman muses on bravery because she is brave. I mean naturally brave. Man's courage is only moral courage, woman's is natural. It's the Narcissus business that matters. Woman thinks she sees courage in a man. The mirror up to nature. You can't see anything in a mirror that isn't in yourself. You can make up pictures, by muscular contractions, like an English Public School accent, on an Irish schoolboy. But they are painted with the grey and pink, and blue, matter of your own brain. The mirror is another cup of tea altogether. Do you know why Bull fighters don't care about fighting a cow? It is because the female charges with her eyes open. I give you my word I cannot recall from my

9

own experience, or my reading of newspapers, one naturally brave man in a large position. And look at the steam-sweat screen that rises around and about the great Heroes of Romance here and there. That's because they're all males. The Amazon she does it on her ear. But then there's the good-natured man and the good-natured woman.

Now, old Brown, you've aired your wise-cracks and they are like any other man's in frosty weather. I've listened and looked like listening, which is far better. So let us play that old game we played many times in the old days. The game of I Remember.

All right, all right. I remember when plays, that are played now as quaint before gigglers in the expensive seats, were played as if the players were the brothers and the sisters, or at least the country or town cousins of the people in the auditorium. I think the quaint toss is the poorest and the most insulting toss ever thrown down before the human life. Wouldn't it be a marvellous thing to thaw out some ancient hero of an ice-age out of his berg, and be so well-mannered and sweet as to be able to sit down with him and discourse of anything that interested him up to the moment the ice took him in the neck? And never confuse him with any up-to-the-minute chat from the surf-washed shores of a Bridge Club.

If people could write plays and books of earlier ages like that how wonderful it would be, to roll back the scroll of time, with no smart Alec. nudging your shoulder, with the pride of a changeling with a washed neck. I give you my word there are more things in my head than ever will be in yours, because I never barricaded my hollow places against them, the way you did when they came to you confessing they never had a dinner jacket.

Wouldn't it be a wonderful thing to be seeing a play about Kings and Queens and bog-trotters all walking on a little hard grass at the side of the bog and giving out their ideas and plans? So clear that everything that was to come after their days would be forgotten by us. Wouldn't that be grand, and you could do it if you had your mind under your proper control. Those were a stylish people, those, who used only the sled and they knowing full well about the wheel, but being too proud to use it. It wasn't the wheel itself they objected to. How could anyone object to the wheel? but it was the going round and round they could not put up with.

But still I remember. I remember a play I saw once, not so many years ago, but it was an old play then and of times long gone away. The actors were nearly all too young to remember the days when the play was in its prime, and there was no one alive to remember the days the play was pitched in. And yet the greater number of the audience had such respect for the old days that they encased the players and their play in a bright white sugar cave like an Easter egg, and inside that cave the old days were breathing warm because the audience liked to have it so, now was that love?

That was love old dusty Brown.

Oh, don't call me dusty Brown. It's very like

the name of a song sung by a grand young man. A creamy pint of a young variety Artist. And he had a dark muffler on, and an old cap, and brand new patches on his clothes he filled so well. Old dusty Brown. I'm not young enough to be called dusty Brown.

I remember chariot races in a circus under a long glass roof, and the way the outer wheels used to spray up the sand and dust when the driver spun his team at the turn. I remember that too. Dust on a chariot wheel. 'I'm the dust on your chariot wheel,' and up came the other lover, with his white silk handkerchief, with his monogram in the corner, and he dusted off the chariot wheel and she laughed and can you beat it!

I remember a small town where no one ever spoke the truth but all thought it. It was a seaport town, like all the best towns. But there was a lake very near to it. The cold brown bosom of the fresh water, and the blue steel verdigris green corsage of the salt water, and between the two the town. There was a Mayor there, as fine a man as ever you might have seen, born in the town and never more than twenty miles from it, except in his mind, travelling in books of travel. He had never been far away for he was a heavy man for walking and an awkward man on a horse, and on a horse's back was the only dignified way for a man of his age to travel. He was about forty years of age. To be carried in a vehicle would be to him making a bundle of himself too soon. The weather in this town was ever of the bland and sweet, and the air always smelling sweet. It should have been a rainy place, for it was in a cup of hills. But a rock island, a mountain island, in the sea, off the mouth of the bay before the town, collected all the heavier clouds and caused them to break and run foaming down the mountain side all among the green trees and the moss-covered rocks.

It was a very secluded town, the time I'm remembering it in. The streets of the town were all just laid down in the form of a letter E, with the back of the letter lying along the river bank and the three prongs, sticking out across the flat space at the bottom of the cup in which the town lay. The prongs had between them two squares, one sanded with white sand, the other paved with yellow stone slabs and in the middle a fountain fed from an over-flowing lake, not the town's own brown lake, but a smaller one up among the hills. And the fountain was capable of throwing a spray higher than the houses. Those on the prongs were no more than short three-storied ones. If the wind was blowing strong over the level of the roofs from the sea, as the fountain square was nearest to the sea, the spray would blow over into the sanded square. And when the girls and boys and young men and young women were pacing about there, they'd get a fist full of shining drops on their cheeks and they would brush the drops off into their hands and then put their hands to their lips, and some of the old ones would do the same. They did not worship the fountain, but they loved it dearly. And when the fountain was in a mind to throw its drops it threw them on the malefactor as well as the honest citizen. It was an

13

impartial town. The Mayor of the town had a beautiful daughter, Ellen, such a simple name for such a grand beauty as she shone with. She had a neck perpetually arched in a forgiving way, which made young men wish to cry, and old men to beat up the young men for their presumption. She was something like her mother except that her mother thought her wonderful and she didn't think about herself at all. She was something like her father. But not so stern looking, not that her father ever frowned. It was just that his brows were set in a line that visitors from afar associated with sternness. The girl's brows were set in two gentle limpid curves and it was by a mental somersault in the brain of the unreasonable that these gentle curves could be associated in any way with sternness. But they were. The Mayor had never received his salary which was a handsome one, and he had been the first citizen of the town since he was a grown man. But if he allowed his salary to remain in arrears, he allowed his own commitments to remain unsettled. There was an idea in his head that he might die, perhaps sooner than usual for a man like himself, and his wife also might pass away, and his daughter also might put off marrying and she might die, and so he would have no grandchild. And therefore he thought that the three of them would be carefree in the bright hereafter. And in meeting any old citizens coming dropping up to join them, there would be no constraint between them as there is between a debtor and a creditor after an account has been settled and a slate wiped. He had been much taken with some intricate accounts which he had worked out on a dry rock using his wetted finger as a pencil. There was a little warm pool of sea water close to the rock. He stayed by the rock until the rising of the tide washed away all trace of his arithmetic. The old friend, and still creditor, for whom he made the figures waited with him to the end, and together they waddled up along the sandy path by the shore, back into the town, passed the small white thatched cottages on the outskirts and over the bridge, where the brown fresh water tumbled into the salt. At a dark and cavernous place where a merchant, as an afterthought, had set up some casks and sold wine, they sat on an empty box, and drank out of horn cups. The box was only a small one and so they had to sit very close together on it, half turned away from each other. But they could drink in reciprocity for as the wine rolled down into their throats their back bones reverberated with esteem for he who made the wine. The wine merchant stood up leaning against his largest cask and singing in a fo'c'sle drone, for he had heard sailors sing so. He had seen sailors in a mass not so very long ago. Romantic creatures, they had no cargo for the port, no business there at all, but passing on the ocean along beyond the mountain island, they felt it would be romantic to be pirates for a time. Two vessels they had full of rigid looking but sulphurous breathing men. There were so many men in those ships always that they never required cargo or ballast. They were ballasted with men. The wind blew convenient for the horrid ideas, and just at the fall of dark on a mild November evening they grounded their hookers, half an hour from high water, fifty yards from the fall of fresh water. Then climbed out of the ships. Their names, the ships' names were 'Darkness' and 'Revenge' just names, they had nothing on their mind about this town which I remember. These sailor men they had knives and hand-spikes and they leapt into the town, and behind the counters, and put their hands into the tills, and some of them were all for dallying about and drinking hard drinks, but the leaders, just appointed on the spot, began to lead the way up the stairs of the houses and the men of the town, who had been watching their going on from the first landings of the stairs, just jumped down on them. In five minutes the pirates, with heads, arms and legs broken, were dragging themselves back to their ships. The money they had taken they gave up to the inhabitants of the town as they legged it for the ships, and before they were afloat. They did more. They were in a hurry for the tide had turned and though they had water under their keels it wouldn't be there for long. They searched every cranny of their ships even with candles for any curious money they might have of their own, they were so anxious to pay their footing to be away. They made the open sea and had very nearly all been drowned for they hadn't distributed themselves equally between Darkness and Revenge, and where Revenge was light and high and tipping over to a dangerous degree, Darkness was taking in the green clear water over the topsides. They hove to and equalised their ballasting.

The Mayor was not a heavy drinking man, two or three horns at a time sufficed him, and he never drank facetiously. He just took what he wished, for he had no fear about alcohol's effect on his health for the length of his life, and the appearance of his death, had been revealed to him in a dream. He looked down on the face of his corpse, and it was of a clean, smooth, mild beauty, as of a lake after a swift lake storm had swept over it. He saw that certainly it was not the face of a man slain by alcohol. So why should he tease himself. The great thing is to know, everyone, well nearly everyone, says that.

The Mayor spent happy days waiting for something to happen, that he hoped would never happen. If he waited long enough. But well he knew that 'long enough' meant long after he was dead. A Circus would descend the hills converging on the town by different routes and the Circus would upset the town, for no townsman could ever jump naturally through a hoop. And the young girls of the town, it was a curious town there were no women there but young girls, old maids, and married women, very settled. The young girls wished only for bright athletes of any male age who could spring through a paper balloon, like sharks flashing through pale water. But there it was, while the Mayor was there, the young girls just thought the ingredient young men were as near perfect, as anything but theirselves could be. And then the fountain was always, in the late evening, gushing and splashing everyone with rainbow splashes and the brains of the town were busy working. It was a town in a beautiful rosy condition financially for its exports were far and away larger, and looked larger, than its imports. A frowsy pack-man staggered down the hill one shining morning, and when he climbed out again in the dark evening notching out every step-hold for himself with his iron bound stick, he had an empty pack. All his looking glasses and fancy masks, God save the mark, and hair pinchers were gone, and his head was full of ideas, for sale, when he could find the buyers. But by the time he got to his buyers, the ideas or anyway the meatiest part of them had melted on him like super fine wax in the presence of flaming brimstone.

It was a town with one internal idea, and that was the brown river. Every evening, rain or shine, you would see two or three persons leaning over the rail alongside the back of the letter E and with their mouths open filling their lungs and their bellies with the fragrant, woolly, ever lovely, unsatisfied boggy breathing of that fulsome, flattering, simple-hearted flood. No man within an hour of coming from that river ever beat his child, even in gesture, and that was all the correction the children ever received, first a gesture of punishment and then a gesture of apology. And no dog coming from that river side barked for a space of time. The children of that town did not rule the town as anyone might suspect. No one ruled that town. Not the Mayor, for all he had his golden chain. It ruled itself. He ruled himself, with the varied tone of the river. Ah, she was a bonny river. It was lucky for the old shells and pebbles within a hundred yards of the falls' edge before she tumbled into the sea. They, it didn't matter how strong the stream was, were always caught up among the rocks on the Easterly side of the falls, and never went out to sea. Never again out to the sea they came from long ago when the earth was blazing hot and volcanoes were pitching sea shells above high water mark. These shells and pebbles being ever caught up by the rocks worked their way back again a few yards every now and again up the river. And then would come a freshet and pitch them downward again, past the townsmen leaning over the rail, a foot on a lower rail. A foot on the rail. So human, so docile. The foot on the rail, the arms reclining on a swilled counter quaffing brimmers like their little piggy wiggy grandsires when they were able. All liquids look alike to man, but they feel differently. They go down, they go down. With some the first floor is enough. With some the basement must be reached before the rafters in the garret shake and illuminate themselves with wreathed roses golden edged. But with the men of the town I'm telling you about the river was nearly enough. It was a mountain still frothing its way with the pure elixir of the high places. Three parts the river, a quarter label and the rest some drossy fire from an ignorant unknown crucible, and the townsman went back into the sandy square and kissed his hand to the falling fountain drops.

There were a lot of people in this God-damned town, most of them different, different in wedges, not in families. Precarious corralling of human beings under roof trees. So these wedges, these different wedges, came from different families and mixed themselves. Perhaps each wedge contained all the necessary ingredients of a wedge, wedge into wedge, and then wedge. That's a non plus. No, they broke away when they felt that coming and starred out into groups of character.

It was a slip of the tongue calling this town a 'God-damned town'. I should not have used that description. It's lost its original meaning. There was a time when a lot of thin hawk-men standing about on their thin soled boots would know the way I was using the description. It's an affectionate term, and as long as I live I'm not going to tell you any more about affectionate terms. If you don't understand them when they drop from my lips, then you never will, God help you.

This nice town had a lot of actors in it, and two actresses. It was not thought nice for women to appear on the stage with a bunch of men. These actors they were for ever rehearsing. There were two Theatres. The Round and the Square. The Round was called 'The Round' because it was round the corner, just round the end of the topmost prong of the letter E. The Square Theatre was on the inside of the lowest prong of the E in the fountain Square. There was no rivalry between the Companies of players. When plays were in season the Theatres were open on alternate nights.

The actors were even game enough to rehearse in the open air. You'd see a couple rehearsing a fight with long swords along the back of the E due

West with a purple light from a grinning sun, and it sinking, playing on the face and front of one of them. The other with the nape of his neck, his spine and his heels as stained as a slit wine skin. Then the two bright boys whacking away with the hoop irons. And up aloft, as demure as you please, the two women players looking out of their window down on the dusty fray.

Ah, them was the times, hot dust, and two or three, no, more, great dollops of thunder drops falling from a cloud rolling away to break itself on one of the surrounding hilltops, and to empty itself over the other side, to whang the unfortunate tillers of the soil, who were trying to grow crops by a calendar, just for the fun of feeding the people of the unctuous town.

And the plays they put on, and every one member of the companies word perfect, were what most people would consider difficult for amateurs. Historical plays, maybe about the hero of old who walked along the bottom of the river at full flood like a submarine man holding his breath for fifteen minutes. A miracle! He walked that way passing the town because he did not wish to disturb friend or foe. Then maybe they'd throw an amusing drama about a foreigner from a far country asking for nick-nacks in the town shop, souvenirs to take home to his ancient home in Hack-me-Tack. But what of it. If you went to one Theatre and found it all dark, you'd hammer at the stage door and the Company would come out, perhaps for a rehearsal, and some in costume, some in their own clothes. They would lead you to the other Theatre. The Round Theatre to the Square or vice versa. If they were in a good humour, they'd bring along some gilded cardboard musical instruments, Angel post horns, and fifes, and round about trumpets, and slack old drums. And if no noise came from the instruments, they would say the noise, 'Thimble, thumble, thump' for the drum, and 'wee, wee, wee' for the fifes. All very pleasant and obliging. It was a sinless place, a kind of a fool's paradise. A sort of Tom Tiddler's ground. But every now and then it became something else and some sugar plum filled young bull man would walk down beyond the dark trees where there was a small cliff above a deep pool in the salt tide. He'd choose the full ebb, and shoot himself so that he'd fall in the waters and have his body rolled away. It was a kind of gentility with them to do that.

There were a lot of boys and girls in this town that seemed to have nothing else to do but wander about and make sheep's eyes at each other. It was a town that seemed to have more than its share of twilight. It was the hills that ringed it round and kept the light back, except from one quarter, the Sou' West, and from there the sun could pour up the gully of the salt river and until it sank into the deep West. Whatever cloudy blur there was during the day, on nine evenings out of ten, the sun would go down strong and bright, and the last old townsman by the rail by the river side, would get it glinted into his old eye. There was plenty of good tradesmen in the town, men who could make barrels, and boot makers, and carpenters and joiners, who made chairs and there was an anchor smith and it was a long time since he made an anchor. But still if any ship sailing the wide sea beyond the Mountain Island at the river mouth had his anchor bitten off by that Great Leviathan, and her Captain knew where he was, he could have come up to the town, and while his ship lay at the Quay, have a new anchor made to his ship's requirement. He could sit in the smith's shanty and see the anchor grow before his stupid eyes, under the smith's hammer, and it was he who could swing a sled good and lusty, and before the Captain had chewed over his whole bag of rags, there would be a beautiful new anchor. As fresh and new to work, and lively working, as a ship newly launched. And the man who weeps when he sees a ship, her big chains rumbling and her grease slithering, and the heavy lumps of timber rattling away from her, as she enters the water, is a dangerous man. But a horrible man is the man who at such a time does not have the longing on him for tears.

There was a Fair Green in the town, but not in use for a long while. It was to the Eastward of the top prong of the E and in the early morning it was often a sunny place. But once a lost calf cried piteously all night there for its mother and the cow came from a hill and climbed down letting herself slip down the steepest bank until she found and consoled the calf.

Then Fairs dwindled on the people of that town. Their meat was brought to them in the basket or in the cart. I don't believe I am giving you a proper idea of this ancient town. The hall doors on the houses, both the private houses and the shops, were very heavy with bands of iron on them and terrific nails. The hall doors of the shops would be to one side of the shop window and the hall inside would have no connection with the shop, except by a devious route along the hall, and then a turn along a passage, lit from the top, and then a turn sharp, and a little slivver of a door could be pulled towards you, and you could slip into the shop. It was a kind of traveller's experience, like a man leaving a thundering machinery room in a factory to go into a little office box with a tight fitting door, and then coming out again into the din. On a busy day, or most any day that wasn't too dreeping with rain, out in the street you'd be all in the middle of a maze of noises, old cart wheels grinding and thumping, people jawing one another, people rolling barrels and dragging wooden cases. And a man wheeling along a two-wheeled truck loaded and grumbling with a hard old axle, and the grease on it black and choked. And another man dusted with flour and meal rattling an empty truck over the cobble stones at the entrance to a yard. Then, your ears boomy with the noise, you'd go in at the hall door and the door would shut after you, and there you'd find the hall as silent as the grave. So silent it'd be that you'd look at the old steel engraving on the Easterly wall, and you'd think everything looked so quiet and settled down in itself, that the engraving was giving off a noise. The movement in it, the classical horse prancing on the stones of an antique street in—may be Athens.

And you'd sit down on a hard chair in the hall, a mahogany chair, nearly carved out of one solid piece, and you'd cross your feet and let yourself pull yourself together. And you'd let your teasing thought lie down inside you for a little while. There in the quiet stillness, and you'd see the light creeping on the wall in front of you, reflected from the wall behind you, for all the walls of the hall were heavy with varnish. After you were resting there a little while, your worrying to be moving would be on you again and you go along slowly down the back of the hall till you come to the passage lit from the top and you begin to smell something out of the shop, candles, and salt beef, or old Demerara sugar. That would make you quiver your nostril. The wild steed of the desert snuffing something. You take the handle of the narrow door in your own hand and turn it and this pulls the door towards you, and in a second your nose would forget to smell anything your ears would be so busy hearing again the noise of the town, deeper and more mournful, coming through the depth of the shop. And in the narrow doorway, standing heavy on your feet, a warm package would push by your ankle, and looking down you would see a small, hairy, long figured dog dart under a counter and begin rattling boxes about, and in a moment you'd hear him crunching biscuits. You'd know that the dog had been in the shadows by your side all the time you were in the hall waiting with carefree patience while you rested on the hard seat. If you had taken a notion to walk up through the house up to the attic where the old travelling trunk

25

with the patches of leather nailed to it, and the worn out boots, and the ancient horse harness, and man's harness, and a gilded body of armour for a Roman sentry in a play, either the Square or the Round, were heaped about. If you went up into the attic you would drag the trunk under the skylight and you'd balance yourself on top of the trunk and you'd push up the skylight and look on the roofs of my town. And you'd be surprised and pleased to see so much of green moss and grass and even wheat growing along the side of the roofs and round the chimney pots, and fine round saucers of lytchens spotting every slate.

If you started up the stairs the dog would follow you to the first floor and even to the second, but not to the attic. No, if you visited the attic, when you got below to the ground floor again, you'd find the long dog with his short legs tucked close into his body while he lay on his belly. He would be waiting silently for you to wake up to his branch of the afternoon's party—the opening of the narrow door.

Any man who ever had the good luck to accomplish the opening of the narrow door was never forgotten, he became indeed a friend. One that the dog expected to meet at any moment, anywhere, in time or out of it. That was the way the dog felt about it. He had no doubts. He had had a good and a gentle mother who, through having a good home in a box near the kitchen for herself and her litter, had never had to consider any harsh training for her puppies. They had acquired all their knowledge without tears. A mass of governors and guardians had not enjoyed treating him like a tree for tourists to carve their ridiculous initials on. How ridiculous initials do look if you suddenly come on them. This little dog had no initials. Indeed, very few persons, and those only late comers, unruly, half-scared visitors from anywhere, who had come down into the town, and got caught there by the tangling dew about the edges of the Fair Green had initials. And these visitors would look as if they were settled for ever in the town, and then one afternoon when the darkness was threatening they'd pack up and carry themselves and their gear away with them out of the town but never by the same side as they came in. It is a fact that any of these strange ones that got the town's dew on their feet, got the idea that they could begin again in some other town, perhaps a different shaped town. Begin again, they thought this time with a grand spirit in their breasts. There was a moment when they felt the dark dew with their white hands for the first time, a moment that had gone for ever from them, as far as this town went, and they never used the moment properly to get the full blast out of it. And they knew there was no way for them to have that chance among the beads of dew again in this town. But in another town, perhaps, they'd get a second chance. Perhaps they wouldn't but anyway they are trying. It was intolerable to see the faces of the townspeople going by them at a level with their own crooked mugs, and the townspeople's faces, sometime blue and pale with the valley damp, and sometimes bright with yellow sunshine coming in obliquely. It was more than they could bear because the townspeople's faces were happy looking. That's not to say that the people were all merry, laughing Merry Andrews, and whatever the female of Andrew is. It's just their faces were calm and waved to a pulsing calmness. Not because they were bursting with happiness, but because they knew always, awake or asleep, walking or sitting, leaning or springing up, that there was a happiness.

They would be going some night to the Theatre, the Square Theatre perhaps. All the grown people almost of the town that could fit into the Theatre. They sit there on benches and stuffed chairs with their hands loosely folded before them, and they'd see a drama of love and hate and evil. Plotting, murdering, virtue triumphant and villainy triumphant too. Sometimes in the play, if it seemed pleasant to do so, they would weep a little in an unconcerned way. But when the play was over out in the darkness of the streets, the streets were only lit by the lighted windows of the citizens, so there were a good many dark patches. Out in the darkness they would only talk of how the play was done. They never spoke of their feelings about the plot, they never had any feelings about it. The play was a miniature event which happened inside a glass ball. The ball could be put away on a shelf, far back on the shelf, and it could be dusted sometimes, and if you peered in closely you could see the play inside. If you were a young girl and very beautiful you peered so closely that your eyelashes would curl and collect any specks of dust you had left on the glass with the first rub you gave it. But it was a good play which was

28

preserved. The most of them rolled down and away in the hollow places of the memory. Those places sank into the inner sides of mountain mines, subterranean lakes, fathomless. Hold up a candle over your head, fathomless! aw, aw, aw, if I slipped now, and the natural wharf at the side of the subterranean lake slippery. No, no, nothing, do stand back from the edge. All right so far. But the people of that old town had other things to amuse themselves than plays at a Theatre. They had Hell and hate and evil desire and they nursed backbiting. They encouraged it in each other. They were dishonest in argument. They neighed after the things they saw in the shop windows just when they didn't have any money. And it was often the grown men and women of that town were hard up. The economy, taken wide, of that town was ramshackle. One time some people had had some capital. But it would be hard to tell in the time I'm speaking of who had any now. They were owers. They loved owing. They thought it brought out all the real human virtues. So the Mayor was not peculiar in having a creditor. He was only odd in the way he thought of the creditor from time to time. He was a man who woke early in the morning before the world about his feet, or about the feet of his house, was awake. And he'd lie in his bed there in the back room, that looked down on the yard, and he'd think of curious, clever, humorous things to say to his heavy creditor. But what was the good of that? When, on his way to see his creditor, he met a friend he would tell the friend the last funny thing he had ready'up his sleeve close to the bone of his arm

29

ready for the damn fool creditor. But his friends couldn't see that it was right, couldn't see it served any purpose to make fun for a man who was only a damn fool because the Mayor was making him one. The Mayor's friend after he heard the witticisms would be worried a little while; for fun to him, as to most of the men of the town, and all the women, was just a faint rattle drum accompaniment to the rolling up and rolling down of the dark spectacle of being alive; for to all the grown people of the town, after they had had their morning's milk, the sky was wrapped and rolled in a blasting blue tragedy of night in day. It seemed so to them, while reason, if they had cared to use it, would have told them that on either hand the sky was in reality flat with serenity, if it was such a day to ignoramuses who might be moving about in countries outside that town. One morning at eleven o'clock, a man, a stranger, on his back, was suddenly noticed, by some citizens looking out of an attic window. The man lay in the middle of the long street and a long knife was pushed through his breast into the roadway beneath him. The man was dead, his shirt and his jacket were soaked with his blood. His face was a useless putty colour. He lay neatly and flatly like an effigy prepared, perhaps for a bonfire, lying waiting until he was wanted. The blow he received must have been given by an assailant who had his two hands on the knife's haft and he must have thrown all his weight behind the knife, and then fallen with the dead man and on top of him. People in the town, who had seen such things done in dreams, knew how the filthy deed was done. They pointed out where the sticker man with his legs spread fell on the dead man. They could see the mark of the knees of his moleskin trousers in the clay on either side of the dead man's legs, and they could see where as the sticker man came down the toes of his boots slid away on the ground. There was nothing in the nature of an inquest. The Mayor said he'd not call one. There was not enough evidence for anyone to make anything out of. By night the people had forgotten even the spot in the roadway where the sharp knife-slit with the bloody edges was under the man when he was lifted. Small red lips calling for revenge. The townspeople saw it that way. But the revenging did not devolve on them. They forgot it all and stood by their brown river and they were pleased that it should be strong with old heavy showers.

It was a town of people always in the prime of life. There were young children there, running and tumbling, hither and yon, and two asses, which gentle mothers had foaled a month before I got into the town. But all the time I was there, there were no births, and no deaths. It was curious there was a kind of stagnation in the trades, the people in the town themselves noted it. No deaths, no buryings. It was no loss financially to anyone, for queer enough there was no Undertaker in the town. No coffin maker, no hearse, no black horses to put under a hearse. All the horses I ever saw were fawny or red and dark brown, and they weren't what I'd call horses. They were what I'd name as round ponies. But the people said they were little horses. Certainly is sure as a jewel shines they were always prancing on the Fair Green or through the town, led, ridden, or driven in the small carts and carriages and floats they had there, always coming and going with their round rumps and their tails switching, as if to drive away flies. But I never saw a fly out of doors in the town and I've seen them inside the windows of the attic, when the sun would warm the glass they'd get smish smushing about eating paint and generally having a good time.

From the attic you could see the sky over the hill rims that surrounded the town. But down in the streets, as a general thing, you never looked up, to get a crick in your neck. Why should you, the same cloud, like a blue indigo island, was always nestling down over the very centre of the place, though the edge of the cloud might be fringed with a golden light—I suppose there was a sun blazing somewhere.

There was a kind of a school in the town for teaching drawing and painting. The pupils were of all ages, young and old, men, women and children. They drifted in on a good day in the morning, and they drifted out at dark, and they never asked to eat all the time they were there. There was no artificial lighting in the school, or they might have stayed through the night. Then another time there wouldn't be a living soul in the place for weeks. The leader, there was a teacher, a fine upstanding man with a red beard. He was a native but had been away a while in distant lands beyond the bogs learning wrinkles, but he could make little use of them, a little more use than the elephant, that grand creature, can make of the wrinkles of his hide which he inherited from his ancestors before you or I were thought of, Jack.

Every morning before the work began, on a working day, the pupils would chase the leader flying round the Statues of the Classic day of Yore which they had there in the passage for the improvement of the people, and they would have him tell out where the beauty of the form did mostly convey itself to the beholder. And then when he was exhausted running and puffing, they'd set him down to make a drawing out of his mind, of something, one of them, it might be a carefree female, thought of. And they would leave him at it, while they improved their dexterity by painting, and drawing, the stony statues, and the barns they were in, and the floors and even themselves. And one time a bird came to a topside window and pecked at it. He was pecking at his own image in the shadowy glass. But they all sat round and painted his likeness in his colours, or drew it in grey pencil. And after a time, looking through his own image, he began to see them sitting there, and learnt that all that looks like looking-glass is not so, and that images may be under images. And there was the ring of pupils drawing the master bird, and there was the bird bobbing and pecking to them. So they sent the teacher out for toasted crumbs and bird seed, and they had the bird in with them. The lightest lad had to climb the high ladder to open the window and take in the bird on his wrist. And three below were holding the ladder, and the top, so narrow, was whipping and weaving

33

in a spiral. But the young boy got down on the floor with the bird on the fist. And the bird walked on the stools, and on the floor, and on the Model Throne, and sat side by side with the young women on their chairs. And they all held their hands out to him and fed him. He was of an eagle kind, red eyed. But when they talked too much he dropped his eyelids. He was a noble creature. When they opened the window again at the top of the ladder the boy held his fist with the bird on it into the dark blue night, and he was gone. Then they let the leader home to his food, he required it, the creature.

There were other teachers in town teaching the people anything they might find the lack of, that is, as far as the teachers were able. But always the young and old learnt together and whether the song was reduced to the little pipe, or the little piper was held up on a knee and encouraged to roar out with the grown throats, I never understood properly, though I was often in the Schools sitting on the bench learning about the absurd wonders of the stars, and why water will not run uphill and other Fated Lives and Histories too. It made the people laugh. They invented a kind of music one time among themselves. It was a kind of rumbly music, two rumbles, one blow, a cart in a tunnel, and above, another cart passing along over the tunnel, and at intervals, where you willed, there were holes in the road and the rumbling from above would come down like sword and spike through the rumbling underground, and all the time the sound above was shot through with a yellow slanting sun, and what you thought the sound of that was, and below the tunnel was breathing with a blue-coloured fog, and whatever you thought the sound of that was. They explained it to me at the time, and sitting among them, with them on either side of me, I understood them, but now it's gone, like the thing you thought you heard and weren't quite sure about, like a man would be standing in a desert place and great cactus growing there, or living on its past growth there beside him. And he'd think it gave a sound and he'd look at it and he wouldn't be sure. And for a moment he would be afraid, standing there with his blue shadow and the blue shadow of the cactus and the grey plain. And he wouldn't put his fate to the touch and say out 'am I deaf'. And then hid fear would pass from him and he would pick up a small stone from the desert and pass it from one hand to another, and then he would rise in himself and stride away, and late that night, when he would be drinking water from a can where there was plenty of water, he wouldn't be able to remember as much about himself and the cactus as I am able to tell you. But such a man would not be properly related to the people of this town I'm telling you about. That kind of old business of the desert couldn't happen to them, and while I was with them it couldn't happen to me, but now it could.

One thing troubled me about these people. I never caught them saying a bad thing about any neighbour behind the back, never to me, and yet I knew that they were full of malicious backbiting. If they drew a dagger from a sheath it drank before it was stabled again. And knowing so, I always was hoping that they were backbiting me when I was away from them up in the attic room, I used for my thinking. An old man and an old woman, who kept a good bold house of drinking, said to me one afternoon when the sun was low and slanting on the floor of the shop. "Go up man under the roof, there's a box with an old rag of a curtain lying against it. Let you recline yourself there with your thoughts. It's a good thinking place. Though it's many years since we climbed to it." It was a good thinking place for me, the sun would come up to the ceiling reflected from one shop window on my side of the street, to another, a shop window, or glasses lying in a window, and so up through the height of the street to my whitey blue ceiling, where the light would flicker and bob. Oh, it was a brave place for thoughts. But as soon as I got up there I found I wasn't thinking, that is, thinking out, planning my ideas, laying one idea against another, one fashion of thought against another. It was more as if I was floating over the roofs of the houses looking clear through the floors of the houses into the basements. And funny things were going on in them basements and cellars. The prongs of the E away from the river, there all the houses had cellars, some had cellar below cellar. The lower ones made, I thought, after the houses were built. But there was no communication from cellar to cellar under the houses. It wasn't that there was a land of gnomes down there living their own lives the way they do day by day in the great Cities of America

36

where maybe there are thirty floors above the earth, and maybe, ten floors, below, and every floor a village, with more or less everything the heart could wish. This old town of my heart wasn't a bit like that. In one cellar an old man, looking like the prisoner of Chillon before they broke into him, was making, or inventing, a secret for War or Peace, turning corners, dog-earing the world, making suns shine where never a sun shone before. And in another cellar a fat man heavy as lead inventing a boat, a shell to float on great lakes supporting noble rowers, with the muscles of the arms attached to their hearts. His plan to waste no time with muscles, but to link the fingers that grasped the oar, without turn or diversion, with the pulsing throb of the heart. The arms he was thinking could be senseless wires so long as the fists grasped and the heart pulsed.

In a basement, perhaps a man, assisted by a woman, would be putting a blas on a jar of father's wine. So that, by an addition of ingredients in their secret memories, it could come forth as any one wine from any foreign land the heart might pierce with longing for. So it was all things to all men and for all women too, for the women of that old town were judges of what they required. If they wished for a strange, seldom thought of, wine from some far land beyond the river, they had it. And they knew when they had it. It produced poesy to get the wine you longed for.

There were poems in the magazine. They had their magazine every month in that town describing the scenery in the land where the grape grew and the pineapple swayed, where the own heart's love of a wine was named. I would like to tell you some of the poems that were printed in that magazine of theirs, but I know I would only be making up my own to palm off on you and I'm no cheat.

My grand town is not dead to anyone who was ever in it for two or three days, except to one man, and he died on the side of it. He died out of it, in mind, body, and spirit, and he did right.

I thought I was to die in that town one dark evening in it long ago. I was leaning on the rail over the river. There was a little man-child about four years of age playing on the stone steps that lead down to the river for the women and their buckets. And this young bucko fell in easy and clever. And I lay down on the wall of the quay and as he floated by caught him by the neck band of his shirt, but he wound his arms round my arms and kicked out into the river, and I not being careful enough, was pulled in. I was out in the river, but though there was a good weight of water, still I got bottom, good hard gravel, and so I walked ashore with the young one, pushing him in front of me. He was laughing to himself and his mouth was full of bog water. There was plenty to laugh at—the grown man rolled in the river. But it wasn't more than forty feet from where the river rolled over the fall into the dark sea tide, and no four-year-old would be above very long down there. And it wasn't that this child didn't know that. He knew it better than I did. He had often measured his height, and his

38

weight, against what would happen to his little body rolling over the curving fall. His idea of death wasn't the same as mine was, not even the same as mine was there in that old town. But he knew there was death and little children went into it as well as grown men and women, though he had never known of anyone dying in his four years. It wasn't that he was such a brave child or a foolhardy child, but in the river so strong with the sleep of death, it was the rolling and groaning and snoring of the river water which called him in to play, not a set play arranged, like 'Jump Little Wagtail', but a tussle and a maul, and perhaps, a long sleep in the centre of the field of play. I had myself set inside that child's mind at that time but I lost myself in it afterwards. Though when I was squelching home through a narrow street, after I'd brought him in, I felt security in my wisdom, in a day or two it was gone off into foolishness. I thought after we'd stamped and shaken ourselves on the quay wall that we would go hand in hand to the boy's home. But he disposed the walk to suit the evening. He shot away from me walking heel and toe very brisk like a little soldier of a mountainy band. I never saw that child again to recognise him. Sometimes a round face would look up at me out of a bunch of round faces and smile, and I'd think it was like the under-water smile I got from the river. But I had no surety, and there were plenty of smiling faces looking up above the stones of the streets and from the heaped and worn pavements that boggled your ways along that town.

39

The old people in my lodgings dried my clothes for me. Hanging them up in their old kitchen I suppose. I took a cup of tea the old woman gave me, and maybe, it was strong with poteen, for I got into my bed and I slept long. I thought being so getting-on-in-years that I was as well in my bed for a while. I told the old people, brief, and brave, what had me in the river. But that's all the boasting I made about it and they, those two old ones, I would say were never a talkative pair.

After that, I was leaning on the rail looking down on the river one evening, and out of the corner of my eye I saw an old man, well not so old, but older than I was then, and he was perched up on big trees felled a long while and intended to be hauled down to the salt water quays and maybe sold away. There were about twenty of these fine logs of trees and they made a comfortable place to sit, and my old boy used to sit. I saw him many days, and he had another old son a bit brighter than himself reading to him out of a heavy book. I never was so impolite as to look over the edge of the book and see what it was. And the reader had a slow drowsy voice, hard to hear any distance away. But my old boy was always listening, though his eyes were wandering, his ears were missing nothing. They were like what you might call cornucopias in a receptive mood.

Well, this evening the light was nearly gone and there could be very little more reading by the light of the sun dimming there among the old store-house walls. My old man came over to me and he leant on the rail and slid his old dry hot body up against mine, and he talked out. There were only ourselves there, for his reader folded his book's covers in on the grey leaves, and with it up in his arm pit, moved away and up a narrow alley to his home where maybe there would be a lamp lit.

My old boy said: "There's nothing in the death. They have us humbugged. Sure half the people in this town are dead. They get up in the morning. They eat their breakfast, they take a turn up the street waiting for a newspaper to be coming in. They go to light the pipe, and they change their mind. They put it away, and then they turn back again to their homes, and between putting away the pipe and turning they die. Or, with more of them, it is that they had a chance to live and they threw it from them.

"Do you know the Mayor? You do, well, there is a man alive, and he is living so that he may die, for he has to die. You will have noticed that there are old men who are very partial to the reading out of books. It is so that the noise of the books may kill the noise of thoughts. Away in China there was a waterfall—a tall great fall of water, and it was so great in the volume that the roar of it could be heard a day's walk away, and travelling people, and people who didn't have to travel, came from every country in those parts, and all of them would be continually and vociferously talking about the roar of that mighty fall of water, going on the way to it, and while they were in its very presence. And then there came a time, a droughty time, and the

waters of the mountains couldn't spare themselves
to make a trickle to the fall. But only one man missed
the falling water. The roar of the talkers was so
occupying in itself that there was no need for the
waters at all. I never came across that one man
who missed the waters but he must have been a
man, sir, of great penetration to be so much wiser
than so many. I would like, sir, this moment to hold
his shoulder in my hand." And at this moment in
his speech, I saw his fingers crooking for it. My old
man took my shoulder in his grip, and I, oh, what
could I do, but shake my head. He held his fingers
so close that if there had been a single star out in
the sky, but the night was too far off yet, I could
have given my spirit into the spirit of that wise
man he longed for. And my old man waited breathing short warm breaths a little while, and then
spoke of the lake, from which our river flowed, and
of how cosy the wild water birds had their nesting
places among the reeds. That was by the rail over
the fresh water. But while I was in that town, I
would often in the morning, near growing to noon,
go across the road to the Westward of the town gate,
and sit on a dry old broken-down boat on the quay
by the salt water. On the salt sea weeds, when the
tide was far out, there was a strong smell, but a
healthy smell that would make you tipsy, if you
had no knowledge of a better way of being tipsy. I
wouldn't be long sitting on the old boat before a
middle-aged man with a short brown clipped beard
laced with grey would come and sit on the gunwale
by my side. He was a man heavily sunburnt. I don't

think he was ever in a house except when he slept. As soon as he was sat beside me a tall round built woman with dark brown hair and a milk and rose complexion, and she no longer young, would come and sit herself on the other side of the old boat, and she would have a pair of binoculars in her lap. And every few minutes she would lift them to her eyes and look out and down the river. That is the salt river, to the ocean. She only spoke herself but seldom, just a word or two to me. She never spoke to the man beside me on my right, nor did he speak to her. And it wasn't that he confined his speech to subjects suitable for a milk white woman's mouth. I had a box of little short cigars. A publican in the main street of the town gave me the box one evening. He said "I have a fancy to give you those little cigars. I think of foolish things". I used to every now and then, if the day was dry and suitable, smoke one of these little cigars and give one to my stubble bearded friend. We both liked them. But it was a long time, so slow is the mind at periods in our lives, before I thought to offer the woman one. She took it like a mouthful of spring water on a parching day. But the next time I offered her one she smiled a loughy pleasant smile, but would not take it. And never would she take a smoke again, even when I rolled a cigarette, and it wasn't that she hadn't smoked the cigar the first time to the end. She'd drawn away from it every breath and whiff there was in it, making it last, and living with it to the stump. The time she spoke I'll tell you what she said. It must have been after she'd heard my companion and myself talking too deep and too long for many meetings, for she said:

"Men are queer, but not half as queer as women think themselves. I wish I had the sense of a ship. Surely they must have sense."

The only other time she spoke was one evening just when it was getting dark. The man must have been talking longer and wilder than any time, for the woman said:

"I am satisfied. That man has satisfied me. He has the power of speech that would give satisfaction to anyone who cared to hear him."

She rose up slowly then and went walking away along on the quay to the West. She may have been just a traveller lodging for a time in the town, if that were possible. Or she may have found some other spot to look out from along the tide—for I never saw her again.

I was standing in my old town itself one day by the fountain and a woman came and sat on the edge of the bowl that caught the fountain's falling water, and she was full of talk, bold and free. But nothing that you, sir, could take exception to so early in the morning. And with laughing, she was lying back holding on to the rim with flat white hands, and in a twinkling of the water spray she was nearly in the water. So, hand quicker than thought,—ah, woe is me 'tis often so—I pitched out my left arm and caught her by the long bright brown barley sugar curl that flew out before her right ear. Most ungallant, but I pulled her up straight and she didn't get all soused. She was grateful to me and well she might be for a rich son of that town had sent from foreign lands to the Mayor a sum of money to keep, he hoped for all time, the fountain splashing full and fair. But what with more people washing, and the expense of bringing water into a town, she could only be a gusher three days a week in the hot summer. Though every day in the winter she prided herself with her shining waters. Night and day then she splashed her way to the grey sea way grey—say that's poeatray.

The day the woman, the woman with the curly locks, nearly went in was one of the special fountain days of summer. When she'd settled herself again, the woman, she said to me: "You're a queer old man." And I wasn't so old at all at that time. "And I'll tell you a secret. A wise woman said to me once." There was a wise woman once. Keep that to yourself and don't forget it. "And now," says the woman on the fountain rim, "I'm telling it to you."

Was her name by any manner of chance Eve? I said, lifting my hand to my head to lift my hat which I hadn't got on having dodged out of my lodgings without it.

"No," the fountainy woman said to me. "She came from a different strain. She passed by Eve in a whirlwind and left her chewing her apple."

Madame, I said, I'll ask you no questions for you have all the answers, and every one would make me look like a white hare in the moonlight on a snowy night lost in my surroundings.

"Sir," she said, "you have the gift of speech."

That's not my only gift, I said. And though I often passed her in the streets of my old town, I thought from those days out I had the right to call it my own town, she never batted an eye on me. They'd scald the heart out of you.

One night, maybe it was winter time, what do I care. I don't remember all the seasons. I was sitting on the benches in the Round the Corner Theatre and there was a sort of a sing-song going forward, and I had a programme in my hand. A thin sheet of pink paper. I have the list of songs, and the singers. No, the singers have gone, before my eyes of memory I'll cry them to you now with the help of God.

"We have lost. We have gained."
"There is a home somewhere."
"Crackle Cackle."

Ah, no. I can't go on. I forget the rest. Ah, there was plenty songs and recitations. One of the reciters forgot a whole lump out of the centre of his poem. But a man on either side of me on the bench knew the words, and called them out to him together. It was a story of bandits on a rocky cliff face fighting the powers that do be annoying the people going about their unlawful occasions. But that's a joke. And that entertainment was no concert of jokers. There was only one woman performer, she had on a pink dress the colour of the programme and she sang a song of distant lands, and the man who accompanied her knelt behind her on the grey stage on one knee, and on the other knee he had perched up a little harp. He gave two whangs of the cords before she began to sing, and again before every verse. And when her song was finished this man led the woman to the footlights, and she went down three steps into the audience and I never noticed her again. When her song was ended, there was no applause. And that was odd. The only lady singing and all the other singers and reciters and performers —there were jugglers and tumbling men—got a round·roll of applause. But nothing for the young woman. But yes, she got something, for everyone hung the head to one side, or lifted its weight in his hand, resting a round cheek on a hollow palm or vice versa. I think now, with those people, it was as it was with me, for all the time the woman sang I heard nothing of the strange coloured lands she sang of. I saw only before me, as if she stood by its grey walls, an old, old house standing by a wide lake, gloomy to the centre, but fringed with dry old reeds, bone rattlers in a small breeze, blowing always for the Americas, across rock and heather and buchalawns, and sandy shore, and wide deep ocean. I hung my head as they hung theirs.

We weep together, we laugh together, we die in one deep grave.

One morning, either in early spring, or early autumn, it's all the same, I was standing by the river by the rail and a man came towards me in his shirt sleeves and he was leading two stout little horses, the peculiar little horses of the town. One had a straw saddle like an ass's straddle and one had an embroidered quilt with a flowered surcingle, and the man in the shirt sleeves said to me:

"The stout men of the town are going round it to view it properly from the heights. What about yourself, Squire, joining them?"

Have I a right?

"Ah, my old son, you have every right. Mount now on which you choose, and ride at your ease and pleasure."

I sought the embroidered blanket, though I would have liked stirrups to rest my feet in. But the barrel of the little horse was so generously round that it supported the calves of my legs, and I could always hold the flowered surcingle. I mounted from a stone defender by the gate of a grain store, and my little horse, an entire of a deep Isabella colour, received me on his broad back with a wrinkling of his tiny black nose and a shifting of his ears. We stopped at the side door of a shop where they sold everything for carousers. You could buy the mug you drank from, take it home with you, and on sour days lift it to your lips and let imagination gurgle down the rich garlands of the ne'er do betters. From the door out stept the owner of the house, his face turning alway from cerulean blue in its fairity to the pink of that programme I spoke to you of. He looked a darling man for a companion of the heights above the town. He lept into the straw bed saddle. He had stirrups. He turned, as he took up the reins, to shirt sleeves and said "Adieu, enjoy yourself". Then he led the way into the main street, and across it, leaving the fountain—it was a dry day with it—on our right

48

hand. Then he pulled up, and around the corner, from left and right, East and West, appeared two small groups. Three horsemen in each. Solid men. Merchant Princes of the town. None of my chatting friends from the rail, or from the salt water group. All handsome men, large in the face, and calm. The hour was early and all looked fresh, bright, and ready for a day of pleasant conversation in a viewing of the panoramas, of whatever value the shifty sun might prepare for us. I was introduced to each man by a wave of the hand and a name, which you never heard me called. It was the first time I heard it and I forgot it again before the day was over. Seven of us, and me, eight, handsome young and full of fun, at that moment, in spirit. But none of my fresh friends were young in years. All solid men with sons and daughters proud of them and wives trusting them out of their sight for a time. Some of the men were turned out very showily, a white circus saddle, or a brand new saddle squeaking, or a quilt like mine, or a green damask curtain with a fringe on it. Some had nose-bags for the horses, others thought to graze them where we rested. Anyway, there was enough to share a plenty with our equine companions. Palfrey is a word we never heard. There was nothing quaint, or mediaeval, about us. We were just on our gallant selves round in the rump and switching of the tail. Some with hog manes and some with them lying down, smooth, with just a gentle wave. All us men, for I was given my package, had packages of food done up with chinese cord tied in secret knots to make you giddy. One man had a box

49

of cigars, covered with embellishments under his arm, and everyone had his couple of jars slung by a strap across his horse's withers.

Our leader, the man who brought me and named me, started straight up a lane which led up to the heights, with here and there a turn and a flat resting place. Most of the way up it was single file. But, at times, we rode in pairs, looking back over our shoulders and describing the scene below us— women hanging out clothes, to blow in the airs over the Fair Green. Or an early toper darting from an alley into a dark shop for his dram, and purring to himself "what of it, it's early, the mist is still on the low ground 'tis true, but the sun is over the main yard in—Samarkand."

While one of us looked back, a Sister Anning, the other watched well the road and one, with a gentle hand, guided his companion's mount. Though it should be said, now in your hearing, after all this time, that there was never a stumble all the way up nor down that day from those little horses. And they had had very little experience of hills. All their bright lives had been spent on the level of the town, some-times chasing round the Fair Green, for extra exer-cise, in the break of the seasons. I think they were not grass-eaters. Their roundness was for decorative-ness and was inherited. The horses looked down on their home very seldom. They did not have that, so easily amused human instinct, for viewing the old from a new angle. One mare, before we had mounted too far up toward the heights, looked down, and saw her small foal, a filly foal, on the Fair Green hemmed in by the women with a ring of wash-tubs. The mare whinnied and her daughter, looking about in every direction, whinnied back. And looking up, she saw something on the way to the sky that she knew was her mother. She whinnied strong and loud, and then they were both satisfied. The young one had perfect faith in her mother's poise and intelligence, and she had no idea of plunging across those extraordinary odd-looking washing tubs.

So our day began well.

When we reached as high up the hilly road as we intended to go, in that direction, we were on what was within a few feet of the topmost height, and the general view of the town, the river, the tide and the river mouth, the small cliffs and the trees to the North of the tidal river, and the islands by the beginning of the ocean. Below us, immediately, we could see into the very smoke tops of the chimneys of the town. We saw people come out into their gardens and dig a bucket full of potatoes for the dinner, and we saw a little boy with a board, with a stick mast on it, and a paper sail, go to the river side and set his ship afloat. We watched the ship sail out before the wind and we saw the current grip it and begin to drag it towards the fall. But a miracle! The ship began to go back against wind and steam toward the shore! The wily urchin had a cord fastened to his ship and we saw him pull her back hand over fist.

We dropped to the ground from our horses, tethering the boasters, but letting the mild ones wander in the bright green field where the sun was shining. But we unloaded all the jars and the parcels of food from the horses before we left them to themselves. There were pleasant rocks sticking up out of the field, many with comfortable slopes like armchairs. And we sat on these and we talked a little, and listened a little, and listened a little to the noise of bees, and the murmurations of the trees and the tall wild yellow flowers, and the birds welcoming us as a scenic arrangement of the good Gods to awake their curiosity and amuse it. They being lazy and indifferent, from seeing so often season after season the same round of bud and flower, fruit and berry. It was not, now I know, early spring, but early autumn, for there was plenty of leaves, I now remember, and only the very tips curled a little yellowly.

From where we rested we could see swing round the edge of the punch bowl a wood on a height, and from its edge, could we get there, we would get a grand view of the lake, though the town might be hidden from us. We planned to go there in a little while. The edge of the field before us dropped steep into an old quarry as old as some of the houses in the town. The edge was protected with a strong hedge and a ditch, and below the quarry again, from the ledge of it, there was a green cliff falling strongly to the Fair Green. We must have been justly high for the air, compared to the town air, was hungry. But I was glad to see that there was plenty of promise of berries to provision the birds up there.

The man leaning next to me on the sunny rock was a man with an oblong face, red hair getting grey, clean shaven, bright jawed, and about fifty or fifty-five years of age. He said to me: "Did you ever pass notice of the effect that rising up in the air has on the value of what you might read in a news-paper? You might see a statement, an announce-ment, an opinion, in a paper on the street level, I never read a paper in a cellar, and you might believe it just as much as the writer of it trusts you to. But if you went up a ladder and took the paper with you, and looked at the matter again, I'm saying you'd be inclined to doubt, to question the man's sayings. And if you climbed up the house to the garret, and took the paper to the window to read again—damn the lie—I believe you wouldn't credit one-fifth of what you'd have in your hand in the Newspaper. And up here in this hour, and in the day, we wouldn't believe one scratch in the whole of the paper from front to back. Has anyone got a newspaper in the pocket? Not a one. So we can't put it to the test." I looked round at the parcels of food neatly placed in a safe place, among the rocks, above the ponies' hooves, and I was glad, at that time, to see that none were wrapped in newspaper.

Someone down the line, as we sat viewing our panorama, called to the man with the oval face, and he called him Alec. He called to him because he wanted him to throw his glance up straight away over the valley of the town to a field on a hill to the North, where two twisted tall poles stood up against a white patch to the sky. They were poles of a goal where football was played, three or four spaces of time away, year or month, I did not catch. But I

53

caught the name Alec. Everyone had been introduced to me when we first met, all with both sur-
names and christian names. And now, by degrees,
I was to hear the nicknames or pet names. For such
men to be in such good humour as they were with
each other, the names they used were imperatively
pet names. I had found all the names I first heard
gone in a few minutes except one Foley, and he
was the only one now without a pet name. And it
wasn't that he wasn't a pettable man. Indeed he
seemed to me to have some refulgence that shone
through him like a lantern, an ever-burning bush.
The names, the nicknames, as I picked them up,
perhaps not in this order exactly, but more or
less, were Pigeon, The Turk, The Absolute,
Pizarro and Carmine. He was the first I met, he
who introduced me to the others. Though they
had these pet names for each other, they all had so
much of the essence of politeness that they kept all
they had to say on a level suitable to a mere visiting
poor fellow like myself. But not so poor. When I
sat between two of them I was on the outer edge at
first when Alec talked to me, as the day wore on I
wore into them like an amalgamated link. Foley
came along the line with his fine shining cigar box.
And some smoked cigars and some pipes, and soon
we began to picture ourselves as figures carved on a
mountain top wreathed in a mist of smoke, and we
wondered if the women and the children down below
thought of us as ancient heroes of another day above
them on the mountain top.

The Turk said: "I've seen as good days as this in

54

foreign places far away, as good to look at, but not as good to be in. This is a pet day. This is a sublime day. O God that it would last!"

"But why worry because a good thing must end. Every time you put one foot before the other it's a moving on the way. Some good steps, some stumbling ones, but only a few really bad ones. Every instant we live and live only, if a word has any meaning in itself, and that I doubt."

"You are roving, my pigeon, away. Any word has only one meaning, any man, or group of men, who try to give a second meaning to any word are guilty of putting a spoke in the everlasting wheel. I have often done it myself. Of course, we are all at it when using the common speech of men. But I mean I have often myself tried to make an old way-worn word come out and pad it to a new meaning —that's Sin."

"Sure what are words but carriers of the emotions, till the great emotions force us back into silence. I could give you a dying speech between the canvas and the footlights that would spur your timbers and melt your marrow. But if I was fit and able, and on my toes, I could, I believe, this moment, if I was down on one of those stages down below I could, with a silence ring down the curtain. But that's my vanity."

"I never saw seven vainer men (I am not able to see myself) than I see here on the hill this morning and why not. We are vain of each other."

"And we have right to be. Fine bold fellows afraid of nothing."

55

"I wish I could believe that of myself."

"It's easy enough if you have the determination. Any man, any hour, can make up his mind to be afraid no more of anything. Put the brave foot down quickly and sternly and stick to it.

"But there is, perhaps, in us all a yellow streak in the weave, and we are afraid it's going to show itself. There was a brave man in the old stories who cried to have a fear put him into. He thought perhaps that he was cursed because he could not be afraid. Yes, that's it, if he was certain in himself that he was cursed it wasn't apprehension. Get rid of apprehension and—whiff, all your troubles are gone."

"And then we'd miss glory. Those heroes of old they were like the man in the story without any fear, I believe they were. Then what satisfaction had they in their battles, if they ever had any battles, as we think of battles. I think they just stood off and made a grand noble song about a battle, or had some broad man make it for them. You cannot have victory on a victory. You must be victorious on another man's wincing. And when heroes fight, they fight as a rosy bouquet and they take no pleasure in withering each other, until by natural decay they all dry up together. And when at last a withered crumbled blossom is dead and like a clutch of dust in a spider's web, then the hero is no more than as if he'd never been. But still I call out 'Glory', and every one of you gets a lift in the upper garret of his stomach, isn't that so?"

"It is so, and it would be a good thing, this instant, that we should all have a little roziner from the jar.

Here, let Carmine, though he's huffed, be my
Senechal and carry the jar round for me to fill up
your cups. Just one round—a lark's song."

He went along the line, bold Foley, and every man
took his toll from the great jar carried in the old-
fashioned style, like a bonuv in the arms, by Carmine.
Certainly, this drink was an encourager. As far as I
knew it had no name. They never told me its
inventor's name. If it couldn't kill this fear it
diffused it with a glorious light. As I sipped the
last drops I felt a horse's lips by my foot feeling at a
piece of grass he wanted especially. I moved my foot
a little way to let him munch munch where he
would, and I looked down at him secretly and softly,
and I wondered did he have any of this fear of fear
which was so bothering us up there above the well-
beloved town. And I said to myself "He has no fear".
"My mottled friend," I said, he was a mottled
horse, "you understand the arithmetic of causes
and their ruléd followers." In my thought conversation with the little horse I could use words as I
liked without fear of sniggering derision. "Ah, little
horse, if all of us were like you." He moved, sliding
along the rim of his eye his sweeping lashes, and
looked into my face with the immeasurable pity of all
the created for the improved-on-creation's creatures.

Pizarro shouted out, pitching down the last of
his cup, "That's the sort of bosom caresser that
they talked of in the days of yore. I'm a tableau of
a battle on the deep seas of wine and I have a fire-
ship in my middle. *Look*, brave my lad, and let who
will wear the silver-plated armour.

> I love Romance,
> I love Romance.
> But Romance don't love me.

It flitters from me and leaves me only the cold skeleton of my own sad rectangular thoughts, and they hurt me when I move. Yes, like the man who swallowed the money-box."

Alec turned his long oval visage toward me and said "Good! Pizarro is speaking truly for us all. We all, and you are one of us, understand that this hour is a mark, a tide mark. No, not a tide mark, but a buoy marking a channel flowing through the wits of men. How inadequate are words, and the usual use of words, to give us what we want to sing into the sky. I wish I had, this moment, the gift of poetry in excelsis, but my muse of poesy was ever to me just a Second Mrs. Potiphar. My middle name's Joe, and when I fled away from her the garment that I left in her hand was the shortest, smallest bit of a leather kilt of a sonnet that ever covered a nakedness. Ah me, ah me!"

Pizarro rose up again and told us what he would do with bravery if he had it. Most everyone then said something carefully, something they intended to be memorable. But, do you see, though I remember so much, I forget their wise sayings: Then the Absolute sang and he was no singer, but he had a kind of a waving murmur that pleased us all:—

> The Song of the Wave I sing,
> The Song of the Molly-go-Well,

The Song of the never-so-bad,
The Song of the rim of the Sea,
The Song of the little round boat.
The Song that pushes her off,
As we go over
The Hibbidy Hubbidies
Along by the tall ship's side.
Heave up the stuff,
Heave up the stuff,
Heave up the pack-ages.
Now captain up your helm
And into the sun's eye sail away,
    Sail away,
    Sail away,
We're dancing on her quarter-deck.
Down below
The long bunk's like a coffin.
But not so like a coffin
Where the wild flowers blow.
I picked them on a headland
By a shore, before
We sailed away.
In the naked tumblers
By a shaking belt
They'll scent and flower away,
Down below.
How the timbers moan,
How the timbers groan,
    Down below.
Some day they'll wither
    And they'll die
    Down below.

And through the port I'll
   throw them
     To their end
On the creaming waves
     Of the sea.
But I sail on
For to-night
I'll sleep sound,
In my narrow trough,
Down the glassy trough
     Of the sea.
So I go rolling on,
     And round.
And you come rolling with me
     Round.

I see feathered green leaves waving high.
I see a fair white sandy shore.
Men like you and I
Walking in the tide,
Calm and quiet.
The sea is indigo black,
The men are ruby black,
Not faint and fair
Like you and me.
Though some of us are black within
Tarnished with our sin
But we can play the music,
And watch the sandy shore.
We go sliding by.
And a little wave passes
     Under us,

And leaves us slackly
    Rolling.
Leaves us on the deeps.
But when it meets
    Its shallows
It tinkles round
The black man's thighs.
And when I sing
"Pollie, oh, lo,
Pollie, oh, lo, lo"
The dark man answers back
With a sweeter voice
    Than mine.
"Pollie, oh, lo,
Pollie, oh, lo, lo, lo."
So we understand the ordinary speech
  of men.
So Captain let her roll
Let her roll
    On her way.

There's a shark
A-following after.
I see his big fin
Split the water.
If I had a third leg
    Or Swinger
I'd swing it
To him in the deeps.

It must be hard
To search the ocean wide

              For legs
              To fill
Such teeth as his.
If we had a patent log
He'd eat our patent log.
But we don't need such things.
              The Captain
He steers by his nostrils
By his nostrils he steers us
              Through the dreepy
              Seas.

His port nostril's
Full of hot pineapple smell
And the odours
Of many spices
And his starboard's
Full of cold sea water
              Smells,
And the Saragossa
              Sea's
And the Saragossa
              Sea's
Not for you and me
Not for we's.
So with the tambourine,
And the gay guitar
We're going sailing down
The deep steps
Of the sea
Always South.
And there are rocky headlands too

And both the Captain's nostrils cold
But my wild flowers
Still hold their own
So home
Is not so far away.

But our cut-water's
Cutting water
Splashing through a wide ocean
Ocean, ocean, ocean.
Flying fishes like decoration
In the spray.
Like decoration in a sugar spray
On the top of a
Wedding cake
Sail away, sail away
No sail's in sight
        At all.

The sea is all our own
        Our own
The river's bright clean green
Inside the indigo cup
Pale indigo cup.

Ahead, ahead
Spattering islands
Tall, narrow,
Narrow, narrow, narrow,
        Islands.

We go through them
Clean and clever
    Through them.
Their parrots
And their bushes
    Beat our sides
As we go sliding through
The puffing wind,
Always puffing
    To our sails.
Then down the hills
    To the South
All the bright blue whales
Are spouting
    Water spouts,
Are spouting too
As wags rolling to the South.

Then up we sail to nor'ard.
The scented wind
On my ported ear.
The walrus, the whale,
And the big fine seals,
A-wallowing in the
Bright blue sea.
A sledded man
A sledding on the ice
By the brink
About, about, about
She comes.
The sunshine on my
    Starboard ear.

Whirll, whirll, whirll,
Round up, and to her bit.
Goodbye, bluff friend,
    Goodbye.
Up to it she comes.

Once again
My pink Port ear
Is turned to gold
Let her feel the bit
It is her due.

Know your style,
Throw your style
    Hearty boy.
Come, my withered wild ones
    From your shelf.
I'll leave you
Where I plucked you
Buried in the sand
Of your own Head Land.

That's my song." And Foley said "You forgot the
icebergs." No other songster hove up a stave. We
all began to shift about and get restless. And soon
we were packing ourselves up on our little horses,
and Carmine and Absolute, leading us along, talking
very seriously together, making our way toward the
hill with the trees which hung over the lake.

There was a valley between us and the trees' hill
so we went a wide detour on the high tableland.

Partly in the lane, and then a while on a track at the side of a hedged field, and then on open moor, streaking away, with tufted bushes here and there, to the South, and I suppose, some time to the sea; but how many days it would take you to reach the sea I didn't know, and I asked no one. I don't think they knew. The sun was strong and pleasant and I rode by the Pigeon's side. His horse thought my horse a superior sort of horse, and I thought Pigeon a superior sort of man. So an interchange of good thoughts kept us easily moving over the warm grass side by side. Birds of the hill bushes fluttered ahead of our cavalcade. I believe one guard of birds took us a quarter of a mile along, and then handed us over to another guard. I saw a pair of bright stoats looking at our procession from over the edge of a rock. After a short severe penetrating look at us they were satisfied, they skipped out of my sight.

But I knew they'd taken us all in and sized us up, wrongly, I thought. I have noticed that the stoat has a way of particularising his gaze. And both these white throats, red bodies and white throats, intemperate natures, were satisfied that Carmine was a leader and an important chief among us. They thought also that we were about something important, and it was better for stoats to forget us and get about their own beady-eyed plots and plans, crossing and double-crossing, interwoven, and so annulled.

I could have sung, myself, as soon as the stoats were out of sight. But I knew the others of our troop wouldn't care for my plan of singing. They were not united in their values of the noises. But not one of them, except perhaps Alec, would have borne with the noise of my throat. At first, at any rate, they would have been united against me. But if I could have gone on as long as Absolute did, they might have blended themselves in some way into my egregious screech. That's what I call it to you, but that's not what I thought of it. It wasn't that I hadn't a trained voice. I had had lessons, and in my young manhood often stood up on an evening in a mouldy drawing-room, when not a man in the room was completely sober, except myself. The ladies would be all sober and the soberest of them all would be the lady who accompanied me carefully, slow, and sad. I often would have to wait for her to come along. And the song I sang, my trained song was:—

> Bright sparkling wine
> Nectar divine
> Pressed to make beauty
> More glorious shine.

I couldn't have remembered any more of the words there on the hill or I might have launched out on it whether they liked it or not. Pigeon said to me, looking away to the South:—

"It looks very lonely all that country stretching away to the sky. A man should be impervious to the false draggings on of hope, who would attempt to cross a waste like that. A man that would journey long there would loose his mind I would think. No one to pet him. The wild range of grass, and herbs, and rocks couldn't stoop to pet an unfortunate man, and even if he had a companion what better off would he be. The companion would be feeling the want of petting. A man who would embark on a sea of land like that would be a great coward, thinking he would lose all and be done with it. It is a grand thing to know of bad places and to avoid them. Some tell me that poisonous mushrooms have a bad smell. Is not that a worthy thing to be thinking on. The goodness of God."

"These things are a serious consideration to me, Pigeon," I said, "and I haven't the benefit of being a citizen of this wise town below us there behind our tracks."

"Ah," he said, "you're as good as a citizen of us and we'll prove it to you whenever the time comes. Now I've forgotten what I said. I'm a talking man. I like talking."

"I like talking too, none better. But talking takes hold of me and drags me off the ground into the high sky to where an ancient citizen of another town flew up into the sun's heat and melted the apparatus of his wings and came down to a rattling death on cruel rocks."

"Did you know that man? I heard of him once or twice."

"Indeed I didn't know him. I'm getting old but he was before my time and before my father's time."

"Ah, well, we'll let him rest."

Foley riding ahead of us looked back and called out "What are you two heroes talking about so seriously? Love isn't everything."

"He knows it isn't very well," said Pizarro, and he was looking very hard and pointed at the Pigeon. Pigeon didn't like this. He took out of his inside pocket in the flap of his coat a clarionet and blew through it a call of derision on Pizarro. And he put it away again. If he didn't pitch it in a furze bush. I don't know. I never saw it again.

Pizarro was silenced from that hour. I never heard him speak again in this life.

We were travelling along this way, quiet and easy, at the pace that suited the careful horses we rode, a long while with our faces mostly turned to the North, where a distant rubbled line of palest blue showed mountain, rock mountain. They, I thought, must have been scored with fierce wind a long time that no verdure should be growing on them. I supposed that was the way in this country I'm talking about. An odd valley here and there, cosy and warm. And then the hill tops, if they were modest and content to grow little bushes to nest small birds and to hide among their roots the small wild furred things, they could live and have their seasons, Spring and Harvest. But if they were proud and stony, stony they remained alone in the cold air where no living thing, unless in fear and hunted, would ever ask to put paw or claw on their heads.

It would be a terrible thing, I thought, to be so that every living creature would run from you, putting the distance between you. A man alone on a raft on the wide ocean has the fishes below him, and the birds of the sea above him, and when he dies some of them will pick him over and entomb his tissues in their bodies to feed and strengthen them. But the man from whom the wild creature run will lie till he shrivels and rots, unless some pitiful one passing by heaps grey stones over him to let the stones nestle to him at least.

But from where we rode those far hills were blue and looked fair enough. And when the Westering of the sun caused it to lighten them up with yellow light, they looked as if they would be no bad place at all to lie in.

So we dawdled along. One, the Turk I think it was, had a suggestion, and he sent it down the line from mouth to mouth, that we should race our horses on a piece of fair clear grass just lying to a Southerly hand. "Ah no," Pizarrro, and everybody else, called out. The day wasn't finished yet, and after all we hadn't brought them out to strive against one another, and I knew well that my bold warrior was too much the buck to wish to defeat any doe, for any dough. Now, that's a joke! a pun! It was the first I made that day and I hope it'll be the last I ever will have made for any day.

So there was no racing. How could we have raced without coloured jackets and caps and over an embroidered quilt? Our horses knew better than that. We trod our way stately, and often silent for a while, until at last we came to the edge of our open plateau. There was a clear space there, and then a little dip. And then the wood, a space for movement through the trees, and beyond the hillside sloping down to a cliff and below the cliff the lake. The edge of the wood facing us was facing

West, and after a space of time, the sun would be burning, making the timbers crack and the rosin sweat. That wouldn't be yet. When we were pulling up, one behind each other on the edge of our plateau, Carmine signalled to Absolute to come to him, to sit on his horse there beside him. And then he motioned with his hands and we spread out in a half moon, the six other of us facing Absolute and himself.

When we were quiet in our places he addressed us as if he was a trained orator giving a set speech. He said:—

"My friends of the old town, the first horse march of this chosen band has reached the hour of the day which marks the day. Up and down this dip behind me, then through the wood to a clearing where for an hour the sun has permission to shine, there on mossy rocks and fallen trees, at their ease the horsemen of the old town will eat, the hour is right. Briefly, citizens follow me."

Then he turned his nag round as abruptly as he could induce her to turn. And Absolute, doing the same with his mount, they lead the way down the dip and up to the entrance into the wood.

> On boys on.
> Such old boys! a Boy's a boy
> As long as he says he's a boy.
> His boyhood rests with him.

Through the track in the wood, light branches gently stroke our cheeks, the small green leaves

almost like the leaves of spring. Spots of sunlight
where the bright shafts fell, and then the clear place
where we sat in a round with our horses behind us.
There was water for them in a bright pool by a
spring, and they had their nose bags. We fell to on
our food bags. Saddle bags were opened and out
came everything grand, oysters, and pies, and bottles
of every shape, and fruit. We had a few apples, but
mostly dried fruits. There were mixtures, all on
one plate, of fruit and meat, that never were mixed
before, and may never be mixed again. Something
in the fingering of the green shadows of the wood
on our shoulders inspired each playful eater.
Everyone was taking his chance in that place. And
the potions that flew after were nursed to make
drinkers forget every flavour but their own at the
moment. One nail driving another home. The Turk
had much to say of all the places where the food
and the wine were nourished waiting for the day
when they should nourish us. And Foley was
whispering some tripping, laughing comment on
every word of the Turk. But he always whispered
into my blunt ear, for ever in those days I had one
side of me that was always missing rumours. And
half way through the meal, the Absolute raised his
song again. A few lines and then he tried to remember
the lines about the icebergs. But he'd forgot them.
When we were satisfied, but still had our full cup
on the ground beside us waiting, then we went at
the playing of a child's game of long ago. The Bird
and Beast and Friend. The bird, the fish, the beast,
the place, the friend, and what did he do? We had

each six pieces of a bark of a tree, and we passed a lead pencil from one to another, and on each piece of bark we wrote the name of any bird we could think of, and so with the fish, the beast, and the rest. Six pieces multiplied by eight. Forty-eight pieces of bark. We were like children all the time. First finding our flecks of bark and then trying to think out the name to put on it. I believed myself the friends' names would turn out to be just shared among us.

I put the name of my horse "Nolens". Each of us, as soon as we'd written on a piece of bark, went to the centre of the clear place, where a wide saddle bag lay open and dropped the bark into the bag's mouth. Seven journeys for each of us. Good exercise. When all were safe in the dice box, for that's what it was to be, a couple of the brave boys gave it a good shaking. And then, up stalked the Absolute, the choice fell on him because he had good sight, a good rolling voice, and liked to roll it. He looked up into the sky overhead, and then pushed his hand into the bag and pulled out the first chip, and read out, in a strong voice. "The Swan, Alec, The Wild boar, The lebeenlone, the mackerel, the fountain at the rail of the river, the goat song. Carmine, The Lion, The Wren, Swan, and Nolens the Horse, the Whale, at the Mayor's House. The stoat at the Round Corner Theatre, the Salmon and Foley went away. The Tiger, the Eagle Cock wrote. The Herring at the river sang. The Linnet, the Horse, the wide ocean, the Crow, on the Lake, talked. The Whale, the Hen, the Dragon, the Trout, the Salmon,

73

the Swan, laughed at the Water fall. Pizarro jumped. The lark, the little brown man, and Foley, that's all."

"What do you make of that, Absolute?" said the Turk.

"Read us our future, our fortunes." Absolute said "I'm thinking."

So while he was thinking Pigeon had to say something. He said "I don't blame Foley, and the Salmon and the stoat, for leaving the Round Corner Theatre. Nor I don't blame the Salmon, the trout, nor the swan, nor the dragon, for laughing at the waterfall. But when Pizarro jumped over my little brown friend here and Foley and the lark, it was surely a grand jump, especially if the lark was singing." And before Pigeon was finished, Absolute sitting there on his green log, began talking out of his throat very level and looking down, on the ground between his feet. The chips of bark were scattered everywhere, for as soon as he had read them he had thrown them from him. He said "I find our story comes this way to me, sitting, here at peace for a draught of time. I find it that we have great beauty near us, and intelligence, and wild thoughts of ancient glories in the skies. That all knowledge is near us, that we may fill ourselves with it, and leave to poor clods the idling by the side of an old battle-field. But our wildness leads us on. And we will not lose friendships, nor bravery, nor the kindness of little things. Our town goes on in steadiness for a time. They think a great deal of us and often speak of us. Many may try to imitate us. But we, because of our clearness of sight into the distance, our bold

74

courage and our friendship for one another, leave our imitators a glory they cannot follow. The greatest magicians of all the days will make a recording of us. To far countries our fame will be carried. And in the farthest shores of our own country we will be held in great esteem. And our noble friends who have known us will tell tales, about us with happiness and joy. We make one great leap and I think our little brown friend is in that leap with us. That's all, and it's the last."

We were full fed with our lunch, and with our fortune, and we might have left it so. But one by one we began going to our little horses, and following one another. Who started the way first, I couldn't tell, we strolled steadily up the hill to the Westward of the wood until we reached an open space where, presently, the gold sun sinking would be shining strong and healthy. It was a spot well chosen to let the whereabouts of our cavalry be known to every man on any hill, on any point of the compass, and even from the bridge of the town. Though from the deep streets of the town all this head of lands was hidden.

Every man tied up his small horse, so that he or she could not stray but could stand easy. And there was sweet enough grass in the place. When our horses were tethered we began tumbling after each other down the hill like boys let out of school. Some of us in twos walked about on the slope of the hill that was above the cliff that came down to the lake. I found I was alone without a companion, though

75

there were four pairs of us. Eight all told, at that hour, and that day. I went down quietly like a man walking on his tip toes to the edge of the field that came down above the cliff. There was nothing on the edge but a ragged poor straggling light hedge of brambles. I thought: Nothing here to stop stampeded calves let alone grown cattle. I stepped through the little barrier and I looked back up the slope of the field, and I saw my friends wandering about in pairs and one group of three, Absolute, the Turk and Carmine were together talking, the heads together as if they were all getting in a word when they could. Foley was beside Pizarro, and Foley was waving his arms and laughing at his own fun, but Pizarro was, I could see, looking about him dumb. When I was through the hedge I found the foot or so of cliff head crumbly and light. I stood carefully, putting my weight well on my feet spread out. I looked over and I saw, instead of deep water to the cliff foot as I expected, there were stones heaped only a few feet under water close in, as if some sliding away of the cliff had settled there. I brought my eyes up the cliff face and I saw a ledge of slaty rock sticking out. I had not seen it before. I thought: Maybe the earth slipped away taking stones and rubble away there and left the ledge. I thought: Maybe that is a ledge that was not exposed to a man's eye since this land was heaved up out of the broken crust holes of the earth.

I looked out over the surface of the lake. It wasn't wide there. It was beginning to shape itself to the size of the river. I looked at the smooth surface. It was a happy blue of a tinge I liked. I could have, perhaps, thrown a big stone, if I could have found a suitable one under the hedge, and broken the surface of that fair face of water. But I had no wish to do so. I thought: I am glad I'm no longer a foolish giddy-pated fat red-faced boy, desiring to be for ever throwing stones, to make a little splash in water, or a little spatter in mud. And I was at that moment a little old brown man and an hour before I would have been insulted, and wounded, to be called 'a little old man'. I thought to myself: It can't be so bad to be old, if you have no aches. Have I any? Not a one. But I may have plenty another day. But what about another day? "Beautiful lake," I said. I made the words, though I did not speak them out, not even whispering, "it is an insult to you that I should not be happy gazing on you so severe and anxious to give away happiness with the air above you". These were silly thoughts to have, a man might say. But hadn't I a right to have them there by myself, only me and the lake and the great arched sky above us. In my pride, and vanity, I forgot that I had seven friends wandering in the field, along the slope behind me. I turned toward the hillside and my friends had ceased to wander and were sitting, slung out side by side, across the hill's face, fifty yards from where I stood at the cliff's edge. One of them, it was Absolute, raised his hand to me. I raised mine, and began weaving up the slope to them. Absolute made way for me on his left, and Pizarro moving a little away. I sat down between them. As I sat down I gave a little puff of air from my open mouth. A slant of sun was pouring diagonally across us. There was great warmth in it, and after looking at the lake, and then climbing up even the short slope, I was languid in myself. Absolute said "That puffed you now, and it would have puffed any of us here. You came up quickly to us while we have just been wandering across, and across the soft grass." And with this he turned his face along the line to the left beyond me and he went on "How is it with us all up here at this time of the day. I'm thinking it's a long while since I was a boy strong, and lepping from rock to rock in my strength, and never a thought of little girls, but always for the game that would take skill and always defying everything, and everybody. If I saw a fence I must leap it. If I saw a gate too big to vault I must climb I would say, 'I never unhasped a gate'. And now here I am paunchy and quiet." And Foley said "You're not so paunchy at all and not so quiet either to-day. When I was a child I thought as a child. When I was a young man I thought as a young man, and now I'm not so very old an old man I think that way. But thinking's one thing, doing's another, and I give you my frozen word talking's another thing altogether. I can lay my hand under my heart, I thank God, and say I never spoke a word of truth in my life unless I was forced to it. But I never missed a chance of holding the floor if I'd get a laugh out of someone, and I was never hard to please, any laugh would do. In fact, without offence to any old discerning friends, I'd as soon, indeed sooner, have a good guffaw from a common

78

mug than a tittered appreciation, behind the hand, from an æsthetic appreciator of good things. I thought my joke was a mistress to be enjoyed by myself only. The first joke I ever made, and I've forgotten it. Anyway, if I haven't, it would be too small to tell you. I made it when my voice was breaking, and it was the way they say. 'It wasn't what he said so much as the funny way he said it.' This is a secret, now when secrets matter no more. But the true entertaining wit is made at the breaking of the voice. Isn't that a deep and curious thought? There'd be a group of four or five boys standing together and up I'd roll and say, very throaty, maybe, 'Fine day men' or 'rough work on the old quayside' and they'd all look sideways at each other and laugh. Fun was before sense. I give you my word on that also."

Then a deep voice on my right hand took up the running—the talking. "I was, when I was a boy, always travelling in my mind, looking at pictures of foreign lands, or reading a book that I'd borrow from some silly old man who never opened it except to shut it again, for fear he'd be tempted. A book about travelling in strange countries among the elephants and the little East Indian buffaloes. A printed picture inside of a sweetie box, or a toilet soap box, showing bright blue seas and palms swishing in the breeze, would have me walking on my toes and reaching up with my chin, thinking I was swimming through a warm sea to follow the wild Islands. They put me sitting on a high old grey stool in my uncle's office. But all the time my mind

79

was far away even when I was slapping the watery brush copying out the letters, and sitting on the letter book, because it was easier than working the press. I was careering through an air that had more space to it than the sour old office where they'd had a fire in the grate there, once, in the year One. The boy before me in that outer office before he cleared out, and he went away following the sea, took a brush of red lead and painted flames up the back of the grate. Every time Uncle Hardy—that's what they called him—saw the flames he'd laugh and go over and pretend to warm his hands before them. And that on a black frost day with the pump in the yard wound in yellow straw. I tell you when I left these lands I laid my course for a warm winter land. And when the sweat would be rolling off me, and I was down to under the seven stone, and I was scraping my arms down with an old stiff collar, the way they scrape a racehorse, with a hoop iron, I was glad.

"I soon saw elephants, and later on again I saw the wild horses. And anything I could buy and sell again, I'd buy. I never bought an elephant. But I always had a muffler full of trinkets. It's wonderful what a little journey will do, or did in those days, to add value to a penny new nothing.

"I think I was the only man, though I wasn't much more than a boy, walking any distance in those parts. Any range of low hills would bring me to another place, and a better price. And a queer lot of names I went by. Anything they called me I'd answer to. And, even if I was dealing with people who understood my speech, I always gave them any name that came into my head.

"If I had a choice this minute, and could cast off a stupid old aching body without splitting it away from my human spirit, I would choose to visit all those old places, East, West, and South. But that could never be I suppose—or could it? But what matter, everything would be changed, if I was not, or again, maybe if I was still the same they would be the same too."

"Ah, you talk too much," I heard the voice of Carmine away down the farthest from me, on my left hand. "You talk too much of old days. I'm as good a boy and as young as ever I was in my spirits, and I never had to go away from the streets of the little town where I was born. I only had to put my little round head back on my narrow little neck and look up and see the wild clouds tearing across the sky from God-knows-last to God-knows-next, and I was enjoying their journey. A Circus poster pasted on the wall of the old distillery would send my little heart galloping in circles. I saw a shooting star one night looking through the window in the roof. And I saw him again the second night, and the third night. Then he quit. It was time he did. I thought he was my own little dog and I only had to whistle to see him sport himself. That was a queer state of mind for a child, and I've been in a queer state of mind, I think, ever since. When I was getting on to be a young fellow, one day, I was down the quays and there was a vessel there, they were drying her sails, and I walked aboard of her, and I as near, as a touch, walked into her hold gazing up along her sails into the sky above her mast head. And the mate of the ship was sitting on the cabin skylight, sorting out the signal flags, and laying them out under the sun, and he began telling me the way sailors on the oceans spelled out messages, me that could not ever leave my native land to travel on the seas. I took up a handful of flags in my hands and I spread them out and I said to that mate 'What do they spell?' he said 'We are sinking, no bread, no water, we've got a **dirty** necked boy aboard that'll never work. Now go ashore to hell out of that.'

"I left him, he was a savage man. But taking one thing with another I would not care to be young again. If I twist an old neck and shoot up old eyes, the clouds and the sky above the house tops look just as good to me as they did when I was in my youth."

And then Carmine's voice was drowned under the booming voice to the Eastward. "Ah," it bellowed, "I was never a boy, I was born with spurs on, and a saddle under me. I saw all the world from a saddle always, and I couldn't tell you when youth was blent into age, if I am aged now. But you don't know that—not one of you. I tell you, the things I saw, looking down on them below me on the surface of the land, would age any one of you, in a moment of time. I saw a yellow-skinned man lying on his back on a broad brown coloured place in a starved country, and he had a long hafted knife run through his belly into the ground. He was staring at the dark blue sky. He wasn't seeing it. He was dead and died a long time. We, in this place, saw in our time a man pinned to the ground with a knife, and though we didn't like it, it didn't make us afraid. And I wasn't afraid of my man dead on his back. But I reached down out of saddle, and I picked up the man's hat, where it was lying, crown up. I caught it delicately, pinching in the soft crown between my fingers, and then I leant out over the dead man, and I gave the hat a spin to make it fall sweetly, and it came down on the man's face and closed it against the cruel sky. I never got down out of saddle off the back of my horse, and now you would wonder why. It wasn't that I wasn't ready to show respect to the dead. No man who ever travelled so many roads as I but would take great liberties with himself to show respect to the dead.

"Well, when I was a boy, and I'm not such a very old one now, I was ever ready to show respect to the dead, I often thought of myself carrying dead bodies, that were killed by the act of God, an earthquake, or a storm washing them up on a dark stony coast.

"I took great care of my muscles and would keep them in great shape against the time I would be carrying the dead on my back to give them decent burial. I was all for good graves. If I heard the grave diggers with their spades hitting heavy earth, or rattling on a stone, in some wayside graveyard out of this town in the country parts I'd go in and say 'not deep enough'. I thought, I was but a child, for a long while, for too long, that I was under an Order to make grave diggers show respect. I ever thought of those things. I was always picking

83

little bunches of wild flowers and making little nosegays, and giving them to my mother, and she would take them from me, and let her dear eyelids droop for a moment and look at them and say 'what a solemn look is on you my son. It is to a young girl you ought to be giving the pretty flowers'. But I would say nothing."

And then with a fiery quickness he reached out his left hand and caught the hand of the man on his left, and so the grasping hand, like a wave, came on to me. From both sides it came, and there I was, centred with my right hand, and my left grasped in a fierce hold. They all rose then to their feet and began running down the hillside toward the low brambles at the cliff top. And they were going faster every galloping tread. And I then saw myself a boy on a winter day, with a crackling frost, long ago, and two boys, bigger than I, had me by the hands and were dragging me along the ice. I remembered clearly the dragging at my arms, and how ahead was a piece of rotten ice, and how I went through it, and it was a shallow pond, and I was wet and muddy but unhurt. I remembered the queer feel in my thighs as I sat on my heels while the boys dragged me on. Then all came clear into my breast as action. There on the green slope I went down on my hunkers, on my heels. No smooth ice under me now but soft spongy grass land. My boots, with the weight of my body on them, put a drag into the ground. The neighbouring hands held to mine, and mine to theirs. The men began to stagger in the running. I lay back all my weight and, just on a little space of earth, a little flattened in front of the thorns, the whole row of men stopped. One by one they released their hands, Last of all they released mine. I sat back panting. and tired into the pit of my stomach, on the grass. The men looked at me without either blame or forgiveness.

In a few minutes one of our little horses whinnied high up above us, where he was standing a little way from the others, with the sun round him like a gold fringe. So we all turned our faces toward him and climbed slowly up the field, and, slow as we went, we found we were all short of breath and puffing, when we got to our horses' sides. We delayed a little packing about the saddles what was valuable of the utensils of our picnic.

We mounted and our horses stepped gently along the piece of level road, placing the curve of the crescents of their shoe marks facing West, above the crescent of the morning which had faced East.

I looked down by my horse's gentle side, and in the soft ground I saw, that symbol of my life a crescent on a crescent reversed and interlaced.

When we got on the hard down-hill lane, we had to lean back on our horses' quarters. I was afraid we would incommode them, but they were sure-footed as we were fumbling, in our minds, for I know at that time, and until we reached the depth of the town and went to our homes, we were in a state neither dawn, nor evening, nor midday, nor night, like straw bottles floating on a sea. In the place by the fountain, and I declare to my God, I never in all my days in that town, saw the fountain pouring its strength up into the air so strongly, we gave our horses to those who came and took them from us and we scattered to our own places.

I went up into my room and I lay on my bed. I only took off my shoes. I slept until the very middle of the night, when I woke. And on the chair by my bedside, there was food and drink put there by my old people who cared for me. I ate and drank and slept again. The sun on my face woke me. I got up. I put on my shoes. I went down into the street. I spoke to two men, they told me that the Mayor had been thought dead. He had fallen in the street a while ago. He had been carried up to his room and laid on his bed, unmoving. His wife had looked in through the door at him, and she had laughed and said: "He went at last". He heard her. He vomited blood on the floor, and then he rose and walked down the stairs. By the stairs' foot his daughter stood. He turned his face to her and said "It is your poor father", and she said nothing. He walked up the street, in the very middle of it, and turned up the steep hill road, and no one followed him but a little boy. He was a fat little boy and his little heart was beating to keep up with the Mayor.

While the men were telling me their story a body of men in dark clothes, like sailormen from far away, came down the centre of the street carrying a body stretched out on their shoulders. It was the Mayor. The sailors having taken a boat and liquor, and bread, had gone rowing up the river. And high above them on a ledge on the cliff face, half way down, with the poor thorn hedge above, and among the thorns a little boy kneeling, they had seen a man's body lie. And two of them had climbed the cliff face and brought down the dead man, his neck broken. I moved away from the three men. I said nothing to anyone. I stood on the roadway, on the bridge, and there came towards me, a stout and stiff built man on a red big-boned horse, such as never came from that country. He turned his face downwards to me and he said: "Will you show the way out of the town—the shortest way—and to the South?"

"I will do that, sir," I said. "But your horse is big-made for a steep hill."

"He will climb it you will find."

So I climbed the road beside the man and the horse, up the steep road I had climbed on my little horse the day that had just left us. When we reached the level top the man said to me "Will you amuse yourself by coming further to the South, this horse can carry double". And he moved the red horse nearer to the bank. I got up on the bank and sat behind the man, and I felt the horse's warm back warm me in the fork. We rode a long while. The man never spoke to me only to the birds. If they gave a chirrup, he gave a chirrup back.

The man had some food with him in an oilskin roll and a jar of strong drink that tasted like flowers. When the promise of the night was showing in the sky we came to a rough hill on our Western hand. There were whins growing on it and behind it the sun was sinking. The man moved his horse along a dip in the road towards the South, and I saw smoke rising from a small town. I was thinking of nothing, when a man came out of a gateway to the West and he led a brown stageen of a horse, by a straw halter, and he looked up at me, and he said "Come down out of that, sir, it isn't meet that two should ride the one horse into our old town. Take this horse of mine and let him take you up the path, up through the whins, a short way to the town". I got down. I held the hand of the man who rode the red horse a moment, and I mounted the brown and rode up the hill and that's my story, sir.

AND
TO YOU
ALSO

I TALKED about Tin Can Racing before, in another book, the book where I first began to jettison my memories which were filling up too well cabin and hold.

Raisins in the Cabin
Almonds in the hold

Oh! Do you remember Walter Crane's heart lifting pictures for those two lines? Such illustrations as those we shall never see any buck, or doe, illustrator make for us again. Such illustrations emanations of the lively spirit of the heart with an eye in it, they have gone away until we meet again, if it can be so, and be the will of God. Like the running, then cantering, then strolling time, to which F. R. Higgins let his Pegasus pad the dust. And he was the last singer of that line, so let us wipe our grieved lips on the stiff old pictured damask napkin of other days and lean ahead into the next course.

Tin Can Racing on the Bull Strand in sight of Dublin, the Bay of Dublin, the lip of the Irish Sea, I first discovered the kick that awaited my discovery —The Tin Can Racing kick. Less Rude old Boreas was whizzing before him, along the sand, parallel to the sea, a light and rusty can. Immediately I hurried forward, the Strand was my aim, no sneering eye lids

93

to grin at my childishness. Along the edge of the broken twisted grasses I scuttled till I found a beautiful new golden syrup tin. The best of all for this sport, as they carry, or did at that time at any rate, a raised rim at either end, which cause them to hold the track. Then I swept the land all about me for some engine to bung holes in the ends of the tin. I couldn't get a stone with enough of a point to it and I had no nail, nor could I find one in any small or large timber of the track. It wasn't a beach in the ordinary acceptance of the word. There were no rounded pebbles on it and I was not then the sportsman, nor am I, I hope, even to-day, the sportsman to throw in the towel and be like the one in the song who was

> Pebbly beach stoney broke
> And must once again take
> The Merry Knockoh.

No Sir, undefeated I searched the shore, and at last my eyes were filled, for I saw before me, glinted in the golden sunlight within an hour of her sinking behind the bog lands of the west, a bar of thin iron flat with a square corner its greater length strongly, firmly, rigidly, sunk in the sand.

Enough—Dates I hope.
Figs I think.
A Bar of Iron By the Beard of the Prophet.

I barged my tin ends on the iron corner of the bar,

and a true axle hole was ready, port and starboard. Soon I had a stick in my hand, pushed it through, my being quivering with the excitement of an experiment. Then leaves from my sketch book. Every one should be an artist and have a sketch book, the leaves, so sound and tough, are so perfect for the sails of Racing tin cans. I fix them. Two square sails on each end of the spar.

I hurried to the smoothest spot of the sand to give my Yacht, I never even named her, most unusual with me, every ship I ever launched had a name on her. I was in a sweat of hurry. I was afraid the Puffing God would fail me, hold his breath to spite me. To wait to be spited is to fear it. But he gave me every chance why wouldn't he, I never attempted to

Blow the man Down,

and away sailed my ship on the land, my rolling, bowling, whistling canister of the sea sand plain.

The whistling of a Racing Jacket.
The whistling of a Racing Can.

And there we are.

It was a glory to see her rattling herself over the little obstructions of reels of cotton, or small stones, or old stokers' shoes, she met on her way.

Now you know nearly as much about Tin Can Sailing as I do. Of Tin Can Racing I can only speak as one who raced his left hand against his right. But fair play is still a Jewel. You could edge them up to the wind a blade of grass breadth by adding sail. Indeed I tried a sort of stunsel boom. I sailed many a can on that shore since that first happy evening. But none ever sailed so gaily for me. Perhaps because the first took the bit in her teeth. It was on a day close to the meeting of many wars.

I am jettisoning memories again because I have too many on deck. Too heavy top side. I must make room for some new ones. When I was young I was often, I know now, a young bore to myself, now I am not so young I don't want to be a not-so-young-bore to myself.

How nice it would be to have a private egotist within one self who would write under a nom de plume while we dozed. Even if we heard the nom de plume through our cloudy ears we would forget it, be lucky, and have no responsibility.

Farewell facetiousness unless it must come creeping back on its own account. That wouldn't be so bad. It's the facetiousness of the Smart Alec who cries out to the bystanders to see what a goose he's made of his fellow. But it would be a gander, for no man would be so simple—smart, if he was in possession of his natural abilities, as to try and make a fellow woman look silly. They seldom try even themselves to make geese of each other. They have other weapons that go home with a more steely prod. But farewell to wise cracks about fellow men and women, most of them are of the "You-took-the-very-words-out-of-my-mouth" Order.

But, whether we will it or not, there is no farewell to those moments in our memories when only one sense drinks alone at the clear well. One sense falls back, another on an instant takes the place with the brimmed lips in the clear spring water. A cold church not as cold as death, another coldness. But our body is cold from bone to bone through the basket of hope and of despair. We see the breath condensing in the air about the organist and from those who sing. We see some mild shaped shoulders shaking just a little. We see grim faces, sorrowful ones. But never a stupid one. The face of the strange little dog who crept in along the aisle is not stupid. We see the yellow shining coffin through the flowers. And when the voices have stopped like the end of a chime, and we move behind others to file past the coffin, and to look at the names, and the messages, on the cards. Each message, as conventional as it could be, was thought on before it was chosen. The thoughts hover about the cards and as we stoop among the flowers in the rare and thin air we feel their scent all about us, and our memories of per-fumes, the rarest and most intensely woven of all our memories, is split away to nothing, and the scents of the flowers of the moment hold us perhaps. Myself, I know they hold in a closely gripping hand, that can never be loosed. We have no friends, and all are our friends. This way that way we toss our thoughts, our common hopes and fears to shift from us the scent of the quiet flowers like never melting white and clear coloured snowflakes. Whenever we open our hands and wish to see those flower petals lying in our palms there they will lie. And children, with children's bright beliefs in good nature still

97

strong within them, lift their faces to let snowflakes fall on them because they think of sweet comfits falling from the sky.

I would like to talk to myself now a sad talking about old friends that were only friends because we both imagined we had a friend, or perhaps with only a word here and there, long sad thoughts want wit thoughts like the young Gentleman of France.

If Bowsie were here I doubt if I could talk to him right out openly. But I created Bowsie to listen to me, and he began to talk to himself, and even his back never looked like listening. And Bowsie in his office, if he ever made it, is standing in the winter before a red open fire, some coal and some turf, and he has a paper in his hand which he shakes from time to time, like an old actor in the days that are no more shaking the sand from the Duke's message. "Sirrah how camest thou? by the craggy mountains? Aye but the mountain steeds were ever sure-footed. How goes it with the Balkans. My lad dost remember the Duke's motto?

"TrTrTremble TrTrTrTraitor
I I I Am H,H,e,r,r,e."

If it is summer Bowsie is standing by the window looking at the busy men and women of the city bouncing by. He has a paper in his hand. As a paper it has an important look. It makes Bowsie look busy. He shakes the paper now and then. He has forgotten what the paper is about. He has forgotten everything but his own name, and that he has a, practically, permanent position.

Farewell Man-Without-a-Shirt you used to listen to me and looked as if you did, you belonged to another age. I might say "I could have better spared a better man" and you might say the same. I must just amuse myself.

Where, on what sea, floats to-day that noble old convict ship full of the wax Effigies of the old long-timers? Perhaps she doesn't float, perhaps she is laid up ashore on a bed of cement. A cruel ignorant human being must have first, in a moment of loathing at himself, then, in a hatred of the beauty of moving life, made the plan which lifted a ship from the lipping living sea and all its deep terrors on to a dry bank and into a bed of cement. Some day in my thoughts those ships will burst the "cere clothes that bind them", and take their place among the blown-abouts, the courage of two hands, the lips which kiss a nail and bless it so that it can never again be bitten in cursings. I saw an elephant under a green tent, in a green field, in a deep country swallow a great handkerchief, which his delicate trunk picked so tidily from the square pocket of an old ploughman's square tailed coat. A butcher laughed, keeping the joke to himself. And presently he felt a nudge behind his own back, too late he turned. His own handkerchief was down with the ploughman's following the deep red lane of the elephant's throat. The butcher's handkerchief was not so large as the ploughman's, it was of a light blue colour. But the ploughman's was well-washed red with a white fogle. You saw them once everywhere. But every fancy has a beginning. Were the red with the white spots the colours of a great pugilist? Did they encircle the flat stomach and the strong loins of some one who stands coated among the crowd of the grand ones in

"The Fives Court"?

That grand picture of the grand ones. But who cares, the good old has-beens warm themselves with their own hearts. As a far wiser man than I am said to Miss Terry "It's better to be a good old has-been than a never-wasser". What do I care, there was that old sporting writer, or a sportsman taking to writing in his declining years, and when he wrote of the death of any old friend, he said, said it always for each one, "When shall we look upon his like again?"

The same for all. How much better than the particular.

Alas Poor Ginger he's gone! The last time I saw him, I was quick enough, I saw him first, I knew it would have been a try for a touch, and you can't get blood out of a stone. So here's a stone, a stone out of which they couldn't get blood, to all the poor old Gingers who walked so gingerly down the seamy path, they're better out of it. There's nothing here nor will be until a bright aged man rises out of the sea to rowel their ribs and make them chuck their chests and forget the words in the meaning of the words, for it is the quickness of the eye that deceives the hand, if you will—zig-zag the paths with me. But I have friends who hate this talking in character. They wouldn't hate it so if they weren't characters themselves. So mote it be, I would like to see plenty of the past taken out and dusted for my amusement, so long as I don't have to live the muggy old stuff.

I would like to see the old Photograph Album brought out again. Long ago it was useful enough, it added to the thickness of boredom, and many's the too exuberant soul had the friskiness reduced by sitting on the edge of a mouldering chair, in a mouldy drawing-room, down in a damp county. Ferns in a grate which never knew the lick of flame since punch drinking went out of fashion, or became too expensive, or the purse holders thought of other ways of spending.

Nevertheless I believe it was the punch drinking that allowed the lighting up of the fire in that mortuary grate. For men for an hour or two every day benevolent with punch would like even the iron of the grate to be warmed with them.

Then the last whiff of the punch died away and the mortuary life, Death in life, of the grate began. I had looked on grates where I knew young ferns had taken their place grown with their brothers and sisters—I am told they have both sorts.

> The Rabbits and hares
> Run together in pairs,
> The poker and tongs
> Together belong

And the dear little fish
Though they can't think they can wish.

Ferns grown into indoor ornaments became full grown and too tattered for the drawing-room and so thrown out into the heap beyond the old hare's form, under the willows, at the extreme westerly corner of the great garden. They sway on life again. I would have this photograph Album on the knees of the viewer, and on his right hand I would have the Remembrancer the guide to the old books people. He would be drest about half Sunday—and race going—best and half in what he would wear when strolling by the long sea shore on a September evening, with a distant American cousin, who would be still more distant when she sailed away next Saturday. And she to be the creature they sang about so long ago:

The frank and free
Young Yankey Maiden.

And the sun would be gently sinking into the Western ocean.

At the same time on Saturday evening this same ocean, with its back cloth of the setting sun will be carrying away on its broad back. This star of the Western World "ensconced"—a good word that!— in a bundle of rugs in a chair on the deck of a tall steamer with a row of funnels.

The guide to the Album will be pointing all the time to the little carte-de-visite photographs and naming the tough and hard disconsolate guys, who have got the spirit to have their faces and their figures fixed with the sun and chemicals.

The women will all seem to be eight heads high. So long, and spreading into the foregrounds, the dresses so billowing. The little noddles, even when the back of the head was woven into a porter's knot or a ship's rope fender, so small the little faces, that it would appear now it must have been with clothes they captured the fancy of the fellers.

Some of the photographs would be speckled with white dots. There was a Norwegian Captain long ago ashore in the mild open winter of the west. He was delighted. He thought the dots were snow and he longed for it. Homesick, homesick for snow.

Arising out of the old family photograph album, I have long thought that if you could get an ordinary bunch of simple people, or people who could, at will, let their complications die down, into comfortable chairs in a nice temperatured room, and then get a sheet, and one of those sons of the Ghosts of old Pepper, which are called, I think, Epidiascopes, and have an honest, fairly honest, man, show on the Magic Lantern Screen old family (just his own old family) photographs and objects connected with himself and his people. I think that would pass the time. And the exhibitor being in the dark would soon get his courage to where he could talk unashamedly about himself and his belongings, and even chuckle to himself over all the remembrances of his own old ones that he was able to recall. I commend this idea to a Waiting World, with so much more time always coming in on everyone's sticky hands. Time which you can do nothing with. You can't liquefy it, put it in a jug, and pour it out, like rendered cheese. As it is like the dry snow of the high latitudes, you can't take it into your hands and mould it into snow balls to pelt against your own image in a looking glass. I say looking glass, because I don't seem to care for "mirror" since Fluff-haired Floss, straining her pronunciation powers to the limit, cried out loud, "The big bute struck my little Cywril on the fore-head. I sore him in the miwwor". And the man in the frock coat with the spotless white shirt and no collar, but a diamond looking front stud, signed her on to play the "Socialite" while the moon lasted.

Has man ever snow balled his own image in a looking glass? Narcissus, soured on himself. And who greased the first greasy pole? Did he walk on it himself, did he climb it? In my youth I was told if you put brown sugar inside your knees you could climb any pole. I never tried it. Why should I? Better let it remain useful information. I close my eyes and I can see the bright boy with the brown sugary knees climbing up top side crying Excelsior and up above the prize. Eating the cake, or whatever the prize was, on the top and pitching the gritty bits down on the crowd. But I always understood that the horizontal greasy pole had a pig in a basket on the end of it. I don't care about that nasty time for the pig—unless it amused the pig. Anyway the whole idea is piggy wiggy, and greasy, to me.

But for splashing nothing can beat an amateur

opening champagne, and stamping around in the expensive puddle, and the waiter cutting his finger, and the spectators crying "you've got a bloody neck on the bottle" and the waiter calling back "to hell with blood. We don't often serve Champagne at the old Bag and Hatchet". At the Bag and Hatchet, that was the grandest Inn on a long road. Every man threw down the weapons of his trade, and every man sang suppled his throat and sang on, taking the time from the hammers, and the saws or the needles and the threads, or the scissors and the combs, or the putty and the putty knives, or the mallets and the hatchets, rattling them in their budgets or their bags and singing fuzzy to the cobwebs in the rafters, or grumbling with the sand on the floor, or slithering over the piercing brightness of the bottles back of the bar. And every cheese knew its own pin. A pin, with his eight brothers, standing up to fate, not a billying pin. Them sort was far away, over hill and dale, up the road and down again, miles away. But still a man striding well in good boots could make the coast where they knew that sort of pin. He could make it by morning. Passing by houses where the lights in windows of cosy rooms went out one by one—and the man with the boots kept climbing on, for his reward he'd get, just as he came down the deep cutting of the road to the town, and looked out to his left hand—the lime juiced light of the peep of day. I used to think that it would be wonderful to go to Liverpool and walk out to Aintree in the night time and wait beside the canal to see the dawn on the canal water, and then walk the grass by the rails of the race course and the stiff fences, everyone, or nearly everyone, to be called "one stiff citizen" and later on the full day. The fallen rider fallen right in the front rank not so stiff a citizen as he lies on the landing side with his head tucked under his wing and only his little swivelling eyes looking up and they seeing the bright plates of the horses coming over him "like flakes of snow". But a race course before the people begin to arrive takes a long deep throaty breath. The hour would drag I believe slowly over the time until first-footers would begin to come, and who would be the first? Not the Hokey Pokey man. He must keep his merchandise cosily at home, as long as he can, nor the half lobster man, nor the oyster man. They must conserve, not the strength, unhappy word, must keep the vague gentleness of the flavour of their trade as long as ever they can. It is no compliment to an oyster to bathe it in vinegar, and vinegar costs money and to be run out of it on the course would be a poor comfort. And to be galloping round the course and then repeat

Do   Da   Do   Da   Day.

Even if you had your everlastings on, taking all the fences, like you did before the Prince of Wales, in front of the horses with a bottle in your fist singing out "will any one have mercy on the Oysterer and lend the loan of a naggin of vinegar for present use", would only make you ridiculous without being elevating. But perhaps the first man on the course would be the man with a certainty and half-a-crown's worth of sixpences from the infant's money-box, to back it with, and his chin new reaped shining like a stubble land at harvest home, while betwixt his finger and his thumb he held his nose and blew it in the grey of the morning, as Adam blew his, and he had a grey morning laid out before him. The knowledge of Good and Evil! without blasphemy, I hoped that Christ had died that we might forget it. It would be right and proper that the first man on the sod should be the man to beat out the ring for the first ballad singer, taking his belt off and cracking it in the air like a long whip. The yells of it in time would bring up the people to make the ring for the singer baring their legs and their stomachs to defy the flying strap and the man behind the strap. If the hairy ruffian should choose to swing the buckle he could sever the legs from them, and leave them standing in the air on nothing, with their tongues hung out to balance themselves. But if any of these things happened it would be before the sun was strong enough to streak the grass. I know now that long before the first race, and the gathering of the full throng of race lovers, I would have been tired of myself and of waiting. Then would be the time when I would wish for Bowsie and the light guitar of his trickling thoughts. Bowsie should never have left me, and yet when he caught the train and sailed away he was dead on his feet. It's better for me that I should fancy a new Bowsie the same in appearance, with his stout heart and kindly instinct buried in fat, but different, oh very different—a listening Bowsie. That's the touch, imagine him by me listening to what, an early bird reviewer, of an early worm work of mine, said I "was pleased to call" my "thoughts". Ah, Bowsie, they don't appreciate you where you are. They fear you. With me, if you came here, to pad pad beside me in the flesh you'd get neither fear nor appreciation. But let us encourage the juices of our hearts with the thought, that if I can think kindly of your imaginary form that is beside me, then the silver of the elemental air will so winnow my thoughts that they will come to your nose, and scented of rose, and yours to me, and God be praised we'll walk on air. Oh such a good air, my dear friend, my Bowsie of the bluff bows, the apple-cheeked bow trampling down the crooked seas making them to lather away a cream of joy a foaming up with light green edges. A foaming Carmine brimmer is grand to look upon. A sparkling Burgundy a grand one must be very grand, but it was seldom I was offered such a one. Bold-faced spectators sitting on a canal boat on long seats watching the Grand National.

> I'm afloat, I'm afloat,
> But while I am funning
> The horses are running,
> The lads and the lasses
> Are going all o'er.
> They'll all shout and sing
> And make the town ring
> With the praise of the races
> Of Sweet Mullaghmore.

Sweet Mullaghmore is a long
While from the Mersey Shore.
But the Irish have their
Shamrock-leaved hoof
On either land.

On the way to the Grand National I bought a jumping frog made of wood from a kerb broker with a
tin tray rattling before the rattling emptiness of his
little belly. Those little frogs were a very lifelike
contraption, with the cobbler's wax to hold the
flail that lifted them up in the air above the tray. It's
a long time since myself or poor Bowsie saw them.
They were a sporting gang and returned to their
home town Tin Tray without making a tinny noise.
Their own comfortable wooden thud drowning the
rattle of the tin. These tin toys have never to me been
able to make such a comforting noise as wooden
ones and they don't smell so sweet either. Most
every luxurious creature, like Bowsie here, likes to
have two senses puffing along side by side. That's
where old waxworks filled in the empty house, won
on smell and sight. Grim and roll the r in it. That
was the way the daughter of Scotland talked in that
old long forgotten day. When the one long settled
in the Sunny South land was upbraided by a new
arrival from the North to the promised land and
the two strolling on the uncracked pavement of the
Strand, London. No, but on the uncracked pavement
of Waterloo Bridge. "Why don't you roll your rs?"
said big Jeanie. "I can't," said wee Jessie, "I've got
lumbago." I suppose there was a true strand when

the bridge was built. But none when I crossed it
years and years and years ago for the Lambeth
School of Arms:

> The Lambeth School of Arms,
> Where nobody nobody harms,
> Thick ears galore,
> And the hospitality of the floor,
> At the Lambeth School of Arms.

> Where Dorafee waits
> At the gates
> With her charms.

That's Dorafee's School of Arms.

And on the walls, when I was there, there was a
black lithograph of a trotting donkey famous in his
day for putting his little neat hooves so quickly
before one another. I had a note of his name but I
lost it long ago, though I kept many stupid things.
I wish I knew the name of that little lad. I think it
was a lad and not a lass. The Lambeth School of
Arms was one of the few places where men punched
each other before pictured walls. There were
pictures I think round the ring in the Blue Anchor.
I know there were plenty in the bird singing room
up the stairs and there was a picture in the Animals'
Institute, but that was mostly a place of wrestling,
not so much pugilism, for they had a soft mattress
to fall on, and the old ringside gluttons when I sat
beside them would not have been satisfied if the

outed man didn't kiss the boards with a thump. I keep trying to imagine Bowsie stalks beside me and yet I know if I could bring him back there he would be as much interested in me as in a hung nail. It's a good thing perhaps for a boxer to walk sideways, presenting the thin edge of the slab of his left side to his enemy—but then it must mean that his right hand has longer to go to connect with the other bright lad's jaw. This bright thin lad who wards off so many blows so easily, probably some trick he inherited from his mother. If I had to give a boxer advice, if there was no escape for me, if I was so hemmed in with circumstances that I must speak, I would say, "Remember if he appears illusive to you you are looking worse to him because you are ever on the change, sometimes you look to him like a barn door and then you look like a church spire in the sky before him. But his idea of your psychology is all wrong. Now hit while he's guessing." There was a noble old ringsider who used to second fighters and give them advice, and the last time he was whispering in the pug's ear a wide-mouth rattler on the plank above called out, "You tell him to go in close if you want him to win", or some other advice of that kind. The old ringsider turned his worn face up to the man on the plank and said, "That's what I am here for", and as he spoke fell down and died. I didn't hear him say it. But I walked with those who buried him, while Bowsie was lying with his heels higher than his head and his head in a sack of malt. The Noble Art of Self Defence, so well named, never forget it, with the red stripes on our far too fat backs where we fell ourselves on the ropes, we still are exponents, if even we were never worth our mother's trouble in rearing us, of the Noble Art of Self Defence. Can you beat it? If you can beat it, then beat it (in another sense). I don't want you, you are no use to me, and poor as an amusement. When I must wilt and die perhaps it would be best that it should be in my own corner, and best, perhaps, that the kicked-up dust of pale rosin should make my departure a dissolving view. Perhaps also that is what most men would ask for and yet at the last moment, all the troupe gone home, caught last buses, or down with influenza and never came, the people who own the hall turning down the lights a warning. Then by a chance it may be that the last of them, the Welsher's Bonnet, has to prolong his last moments by removing his garments one by one, until he stands before the old stay-them-all-outs and stops only at the point of decency in his singlet and his slip, being an amateur, and in the last moment all are amateurs, he daren't show his navel. And so he appeals to the mercy that is in the hearts of all the human race for the naked human. Partly because they bring fear they are so slithery, and if they are wicked you can't get a grip on them. That is why the Chinese bandit Bad Boy having produced civilization to the highest point of civilization and sophistication, when it falls over on the other side, stript to the golden buff, then, to keep a hold on the skins of the earthy, he puts fish hooks in his pig-tail. The Chinese, the French and the Irish are undefeatable. They always went out to fight and they were always beaten to a standstill. But they always drove their pickets in. They only have to advance slowly now putting one foot before the other, the way young children when tired are kept on the trail "keep on just putting one foot before the other, my darling dear," and suddenly the sky around them becomes lighter.

The dough-headed people of the world are receding. If they are too feeble to tuck their tails between their legs each tucks his neighbour's tail and so we call it another day. One day we will be so wise about our possessions that we won't want to wear them all at once, and so we may be able to contemplate pugilists fighting for glory and soft cash without any idea of having them filmed as they fight. The substitution of the celluloid memory of an event for a chancy human and private memory weakens the event itself, and presently you have a visual entertainment that is more than a quarter ballet—like Association football. And when it's seventy-five per cent ballet it still won't be straight ballet. And about that time a trap-door will open in the middle of the playing-field and the referee squealing on his whistle will disappear down below followed by the players. Cricket being a minuet, and dignified with its great age before the films came along, may last longer, and also because the minuet is such a particularly up-stage sort of dance. If Cricket had ever been linked to the cotillion it would have been different, even so "the smart cotillion unsuited to the million" would have remained unsullied by the flickings of the screen. And yet the screen didn't mean to do any one any harm only to make some money for the sportsmen connected with the screen, and when the last word is spoken it is the fast shutter which is the real cause of the spoiling of a game. When I see "a still" in a newspaper of Mother's Boy popping straight up into the air to meet a football with his round head and bounce it, while his friends and foes make little harlequinade posturing right and left. When I see this I wish I had never opened that newspaper.

Boxing when I first saw it was for those who appreciated, at least the appearance of, an olden day. The cunningly knotted handkerchief round the waist. The fighting small clothes coming well down below the calf of the leg. The light high-lows. Often the fighter in the ring might have slid from the coloured print of the old-timer hung on the wall, and among the ringsiders your eye would rest awhile with affectionate interest on a coachman-looking overcoat, double sewn and overlapped at all the seams, and almost every part would be of a kind peculiar to the feeling of the nob it covered. The low-crowned billycock with the curly brim side by side with the high-domed wide and flat-brimmed built of as hard a felt as the billycock. A few broadly checked caps were beginning to creep about worn very markedly over the eyes, to shade eagle glances from the yellow flaring gas jets up above the world so high. Yellow gaslight made the old roped magic circle hum and brim with excitement for me, an excitement which never got me by the breast and shook me so well under the white light. For one

thing, under the gaslight the men's bodies took a
more fighting colour and their shed blood took a
more Burgundian tinge.

>   The dark Burgundian wine
>   That would make a fool divine.

Every good colour was thrown down for the fighting
men and

>   In Eighteen-eighty-nine
>   Upon an emerald plain
>   John L. Sullivan,
>   The Strong Boy of Boston,
>   Fought seventy-five red rounds
>   With Jake Kilrain.

By quotation, you may remember the heroic history
best. But by quotation we surely do live in it best.

    Mutt: "How old is Hortense?"
    Jeff: "She was playing Camille in Sacramento
           the night Corbett fought Chyonskie on the
           barge."

I saw a young boxer once beautifully turned out
with a pair of lovely fighting boots given him by his
sweetheart. After three rounds of gentle glove flap-
ping he sat in his corner and he was laughing. When
the second pushed him through the ropes towards
the dressing-room he said to him, "Don't ever come

here again". He was too well turned out to make history. Costume must not be too well chosen. The fortune of the stars, the weather, and the hour must decide, and that perhaps at the last moment, between the cobble-stones and the sawdust. Carton in his slippers wouldn't have the power to worry our old hearts as Carton in his cold top boots on the ladder, one rung up one rung down, can do every time we see Frederick Barnard's drawing of him in a dingy old junk shop window. Clothes don't make the man. But they give the man a chance. I do not put everything on the boots, it was the long-skirted coat that clothed the Revolution which helped the boots to swing about the stage. Nothing lasts but for a time. Still Irving's hop-and-go constant walk suited those boots and that long coat so well that, with better luck, a great block of drama might have lived about them even to this day and beyond it. As soon as we get a good carrying costume somebody has to come along and change it. Perhaps it's just shop-keeping and the costumiers want to sell something new instead of hiring out the old all the time. Ah well, I hope we don't always get what we deserve. I hope we're not as bad as all that, not as bad as all we get. No man on earth was so bad as some of the hotel table d'hotes he would be liable to have slapped down before him. Still it must be a great moment, a pulling back from the craggy brink, when the weary pugilist, weary of wandering round inside ropes which never befriend him, to see after some lucky punch, where his lucky angel pushed out his fist, his opposite warrior lying broad on his back, satisfied to be beat to the wide, with no intention of opening his eye while the one, two, three, four, five, six, seven, eight, nine, ten simple multiplication is breathing up the air. What a moment—old troubles forgotten for a little while. How peaceful the avenue of our futures would look if we count out all our too vitiating care in a count of ten. "You're out," "you're out," "you're out," go home to your noisome tenement and let me always circle away from it. And how that lathy coachman in his long black Newmarket, with the crimson carnation in the lapel, how he circled away round the big pond in the park, on the Sunday before Chestnut Sunday, with his four dark bays rattling to their beckoning nose-bags, and their stables, as did he himself. He smiled down on me in gentle pity as I sat beside him on the box. He was sighing to himself lightly in his middle throat, and leaning his chin down into the comforting folds of his white four-in-hand cravat with its splinter-bar pin. He was as happy then as ever he was though he lived into more exciting moments. And now he's old, doubled up, like a horseshoe twisted by a professional strong man, and breathing like a fish in an aquarium, but if he was to hear a horse whinnying in a field he would rub a finger down the side of his nose and then pinch his old knees and wish for sleep. I saw him once again, once only to know him, though I may often have passed him changed with the passing years. I do not want to think of those coaching curls before the ears with silver lines among the raven's feathers. But perhaps he has had sense enough to give the something out of a bottle like the young man in the song. The second time I saw him he had been a passenger, urbane, uncritical, driven down to Epsom Downs by an amateur and there'd been a spill. No one, man or beast, got more than a shaking. But the amateur coachman was sad about it and apologetic. Sad, for it was his off day, or the off day for the watcher of his luck. The inn he had brought his professional whip to was uneven, profuse in the wrong place, on the tables everywhere were large glass flat dishes full of piccalilli. Perhaps the owner was an old East-ender, who thought every one must think our earthly paradise is surely scented with fried fish, piccalilli and paragoric, like the New Cut in the days of old when we were boys, and gave an atmosphere as he would have it for himself. But the long bar of the Criterion did not smell of piccalilli, and the amateur whip knew that and knew that the professional couldn't appreciate the New Cut. The amateur was low in himself. It was perhaps the cruelty of the buck in the ever season of the deer park, but my professional whip was bland and graceful. He stood over me where I lunched soberly and he admired himself in the looking-glass on the coffee-room chimney-piece, and he pulled his tie straight; it was a stiff long-ended silver grey bow, not the billowy four-in-hand of his working hours, and he sang softly, but not so softly that I did not hear.

> She loves me,
> I know that she loves me.

Ah, Mars in his glory rattling a song in his gold helmet. Saturn registering disdain. I saw him but a few hours ago in a point-to-point in the county of Dublin. Sleet on the hills, mud and water on the course, he was finishing fourth. Orange jacket, green cap, aloft on a musical comedy queen named after music, and she was blowing hard; they were a long way fourth, drenched and muddy. He may perhaps himself have helped her to get even as near as she did to a place for his name carried wings. But he was unimpressed with that day in February of this year, and six lengths from the post, and the Judge in his cart, he lent away and blew his nose as Adam blew his, with his fingers—a farewell to point-to-point.

Of all the gifts my Fairy Godmother gave me I cannot tell myself which I am most thankful for. But there is one I have loved long, and though sometimes my love cooled, I found it at my heart and throat again. It is that gift of the gab, and because I love it so, I think it a golden gift, and because I have had it for my use I think it very large and fine. But I think now I will offer it, not wittily saying "I'm not looking a gift in the mouth", back to my Fairy Godmother so that she can give it to some one younger in talking. And if she says, "Well, take something else, some other gift in exchange", if she says that, I'll be dumb, for I don't know what to ask for except fortune, and I am half afraid Fairy God-mothers don't give those sort of gifts.

And if I could pass on gifts I don't think my kind old watcher could give the Man-Without-a-Shirt—a shirt, and would I think it wise, if I could do so, to wish a shirt on him? Perhaps the best gift for him is the one he already got from his own Fairy God-mother, in his cradle before they fitted him with his first shirt, if he ever had a first shirt, to be free of shirt desire, or the gift of being able to imagine soft magnificent shirting to cover his back and sides. Perhaps instead of throwing off the cloak of the gift of the gab it would be better to fix on some one, the Man-Without-a-Shirt perhaps, and convince them that they are gifted with a joy in listening. Though what they do most likely is to close up the stuttering shutters of their face and toss their mind up into the round ceiling, up high, aloft among the rolling fat cupids and the fat clouds up above the highest gallery——

The parasol of the auditorium. And think what a trouble the production of the appearance of the gift gives the ring-master of the circus. But that isn't the gab that's the guff "you hignorant fellow whatever hever har you hat Halfonse!" And the sad-faced clown stumbles along on the ring-master's left, while up above the ring-master, on his right, sits the beauti-ful girl with her small toes crossed there on the back of a grand old cream horse. That beautiful girl with her wide short skirt spread out looks like a crisp new bouquet upside down. Her narrow coiffure on the top of her head, her corsage, make the stem of the bouquet, and her pink-white legs are lilies from the centre of the bouquet along the old horse's side. I used to think that strongly aspirated speech of the ring-master's was his own idea of refinement. But I know now that it is a tradition handed down a hundred and thirty years from the man who first found it got the audience where they lived. Those that thought it superior speech were pleased to have such a ring-master before them. Those that thought the poor devil knew no better were pleased to feel superior but kind, I should worry. A great sign of the settled boy is being able to get a sweet melancholy pleasure out of remembering old slang. "I should worry!" Here's myself and the Man-Without-a-Shirt sitting on a comfortable rock facing a western sea with a tall starry-eyed sky before us. Oh, but what is that shadow form to the left of the shirtless? It is the figure of fun called Bowsie. "Baron," I say, "is that Bowsie snuggling on your left?" And the Baron says, "No one 'ere, Captain, unless you say so". "Bowsie as I live," I call out making it so. "Very well, Captain, have it your own way; Bowsie it is." But I know, in my undeceivable bones, that it's but the shadow of a lump of pine root from an old bog, washed to sea down the coast, and then washed back to land again, here in this bay, an effort of the irrepressible Gulf Stream. If we could pipe the Gulf Stream into Ireland we'd have constant hot water. A pipe dream. I talk to amuse myself and only on the off chance after the event will I give a thought to amusing the shadow of Bowsie. Well, he amused me often enough in spite of everything. He was one of nature's brave ones as nearly naturally brave as any man can be. But very cautious except when his blood was up and then, fearing himself, he took alcohol, a full drink quietly, for well he knew that to himself, though not to all men, the lanes in

Bacchus Land were pleasant, thoughtful, meandering and peaceful.

There are men walking this earth to-day unbattered, and still insurable, because Bowsie sidetracked the drinking of their blood for the blood of John Barleycorn. Let Bowsie rest, Baron, let you sit in close to me and con the team you who saw so much of life from the coach-top. I have played horses for every fibre of my little body, little fat body, when I was a small round boy. I had four boys in front of me all harnessed with string, and I had reins, and I shook 'em up and galloped—I think that word should always be spelt for style with a u, galluped—I galluped them. And now, Baron, I'm driving a dashing variegated team of horses, very fast, full manes tossing, a piebald and a rich brown on the pole, and in front near side a silver-grey, like a salmon's belly, beside him an entire coal-black out of a circus, and he chasing the swallow up hill and down dale, by lake and river, by stony mountains and heathery hills. And those sixteen hooves aren't rattling any noise not to us up here, maybe we are deaf to all the world to all but myself and yourself talking or thinking. But eyes are bright, and four lots of lovely ears are pricking forward and lying back, and all the time the long bodies undulating up the hills and down the long slopes and bog lands to the left hand, and to the right a woody island on a lake with reeds in some of the little bays and little mothers of fuzzy black balls of feathers a zig-zagging through those reeds.

There was a song long ago—The Rocky Road to

Dublin—it went with a dance and a battering of boots. But if this is the road to Dublin it's not too damn rocky. Its sand is whitened with limestone.

One time, in another country, when the land was a heavy deep putty-like clay, I found I had "the office" —that is old-fashioned square-tailed slang, sporting grandfathers' slang, grandfathers of the Corinthians —the word—the hint for the race meeting, in the West country of London.

Oh, so many bookmakers, one had such short hair that it made everyone who saw it laugh. But the wise ones entrusted him with their kisses on the lips of chance, for on the principle of my old friend's advice, "always travel by a coach which has had an accident the day before", twice running tosses are no good they spell eclipse.

There was a canal near that little racecourse, just as there was one beside the Grand National, with beautiful little covering bridges near which the midges used to crowd, and twist about, waiting for the honest Artist, with his little folding stool and his easel to come to them, to be bothered. In spite of the secrecy of this race meeting the three-card men, and the minor lumberers, got there. But I never knew them to do too well at those races. I think, though the natives of the land might look and speak with simplicity, they had a kind of extra metropolitan cunning, scratched out of a hedge in the winter when the east wind blew over their heavy land. There were some fine tall elms near the paddock, and not far away some huge timber barns, lumping up into the air, rising above the flat fields, they gave a lifting to the eyelids. A small river meandered through the country. There was a water-jump on the course, and by a corner of the road heavy timber rails and a clear pool. These dreadful nightmare questions: "For what would you sell your right, while your life lasts, to see, or even to only hear, the running of a little river?" "While your life lasts" is perhaps not enough, for you might say what I lose here may be added to me in far greater measure in that Great Paradise. The old preacher nearby at his own last turnpike gate held his short arms out towards the whey and pink-faced congregation and moaned to them, "Oh, could I but tell you all the joyful happiness that is prepared for you in heaven! Oh, could I make you understand and believe me!"

But far away, well not so many miles as the crow flies, from these sweet sad corners of a small brook, between the railings round the ring on a sophisticated racecourse, an exploding faced man pulling at his collar-stud, where it is too tight for him, in an apoplexy of desire to be on a good thing before it evaporated its win into other men's pockets, screams, "Listen, listen. Five musheyrooms the Goat".

At another race meeting, a trotting race meeting where those jig-actioned worries of the human heart puss-cat-minded, raw-boned, throw-footed, creeping and swinging, sub-human, extra equine, snorting pacers, and trotters, wafted themselves round and round the cinders. There a tall man, in a stately linen coat to his heels striped red and white,

flapped the flap of a tent and called to all citizens
within reach of his voice:

> Come and see,
> Come and see the wonder,
> The wonder of the world,
> The Goat.

Why I never saw it I cannot now tell, perhaps I had
to make across the hedges and the ditches, for a
railway, or perhaps I had, even in my youth, the
encrusted sense of the old, which lets a mystery that
sounds good rest on the shallows of its sound—but
I never saw the

> Wonder of the World,
> The Goat.

I could have seen it for thrupence.

I always keep painting again for my pleasure the
picture photographed in my mind—a mere digres-
sion into my early youth. My first acquaintance with
the quick, ready to tongue, parody. I read in the old
smokeroom of the old house from the Bab Ballads:

> Oh that day of sorrow, misery and rage
> I shall carry to the Catacombs of Age,
> Photographically lined
> On the tablet of my mind.

And the Elder, gazing at me with a solemn look in
his pale blue eyes and fingering the large horse-shoe
pin in his white linen piqué cravat, said:

Photographically lined
On a tender place behind
When yesterday has faded from its page.

I was gazing with my one great eye and my not so great one at the scene of mountain, forest, and lake, on the strong wood which made the end of a shooting gallery on another racecourse. And the owner of the shooting gallery, a very dark, very handsome man, with sweeping brown moustache, flashed his white teeth at me in an agreeable way, and said, "The man who painted that ought to have a first-class ticket to Hades". I didn't want to do the memory of a brother of the brush any harm, so I tried to willow myself to suggest that I didn't think it as bad as all that. But the shadowy railway porter on the foggy platform said, "Hades? No, Sir, you passed Hades a while back. This is ——," and then the train, in the dream, rolled on and the empty-faced man opposite you opened the window and struck a match on the wall of the black night. He pulled the window up again and seemed satisfied. These dreams must only end, it is understood, with "and then I woke up". But why wake up at one time more than another. Playgoers, what a nice name that is for a theatre audience, fidget their little minds when the last act doesn't completely bulldose, then awake. It's then the second safety curtain should be lowered with upon it the words:

Go Home and Awake!

It must be a cavernous, and yet glorious, moment when the author, after a series of piercing cries of "Author", comes on the stage and finds one hardy sportsman alone in the gullet of the auditorium, all the others, men, women and nut-headed daughters, gone home. The author would say, "I thank you, Sir, and audience for your kindness, and for staying to express it. I am indeed deeply moved. It's not by the numbers of appreciable skulls we are rolled to splendour, but by the intensity of the appreciation of one skull." And the audience says, "And I thank you for your play, and for nowhere in it, or since, telling me what it is all about. And there I leave you wrap a muffler round your neck going home, Sir, for the night is cold." . . . Sometimes it comes on me that it would be better if in whirling my thoughts, the way you can whirl toffee, hot and sticky, out of the toffee-pot, or the way glass-blowers twist up a nubble of melted glass on a bar of iron, if in whirling my thoughts out of my skull, and down on to the cold paper, I should not think of any listener. Bowsie I sacked. And the Man-Without-a-Shirt, I don't know whether he's here listening with his ear open or not. I should perhaps think of no one unless, unless, ah yes, I would wish to remember that great one, I can hardly be said to know, or even to have known him—the GOOD BOY. I read about him in a book, or in a review of a book, and this is how, as well as I can remember it, they spun his description:

"He was one of the good boys,
    One of the all rights,
    One of the blue bloods,
    One of the get there, stay there,
    Win theres—
    One of the picked."

That's good enough, and the starter at the old
running ground in the far East of London stuffing
newspaper wads, torn from a bunch of newspapers
in his side pocket, into the muzzle of the old horse
pistol he started the runners with, men, and the little
grey trotting asses. He was a shiner that starter! A
faun Newmarket down to his heels, and boots with a
patent golosh, and he had a patent right fist, and in
a corner he had to use it, and he scored.

He was a sad-faced man. He must have looked on
many sorrowful things in his days. The yellow-
brown brick houses about his sunny ground were
dingy with sorrow. More tears were shed behind
the hard lace curtains of the front rooms of those
houses than beer was swallowed there. Once in a
long while they rushed the can. The jug came from
the Crooked Billet straight and was passed round a
gloomy party in a frigid parlour. But at the Billet itself
the even flow of the strong-bodied mild-flavoured
went steadily on cruising by the rounded headlands
of the country of forgetfulness. There men agreed
with each other, and why not, they were lapped on
the same waves. Though perhaps, every ten days or
so, some too strong navvy would see his pipe fall
from the bar, and instead of falling where the saw-

dust was thick, fall on the nail in the exposed floor board, where some innovator had once tried the effect of a sparkling patterned oilcloth. The pipe lies broken in neat halves, showing dark grey, well seasoned, inside finished, never more to comfort its owner. A happening like that, a blow from an ugly chance right in the middle of a happy afternoon sours a man's throat if there is not a wise Confucian there with a wise saw to wrap up shock and sorrow, a difficult pair to handle on a tongue, but easy to tangle there. He is here. He steps out on the saw-dust, humanity's love shining from his dreaming eye. He says, "Do you mind Mickey Barlow after he lost the colouring clay competition, and took up with growing a vegetable marrow to win a gold medal that they said they'd give to the biggest of the season, and Barlow he was feeding that marrow night and morning, and fanning the sun off it, and encouraging the rain if it was a warm rain. And he had himself photographed standing by it. And another week and he had himself done again standing by it. And the marrow was looking bigger nor ever. But stand from under he was looking smaller. Parson up top side came and had a look, and he said, 'It's the contrast'. Contrast me old hat! A police-man had a look at it and he said he knew he'd experience. He said, 'It's the man that's shrinking'. And it's a fact the last time they took the photo of the marrow, the night before the show, they couldn't find Barlow—I never seen him since." And a new little mustang of a pipe began to break itself in, willingly, in the hopeful, caressing lips of the late owner of the broken crucible of shag. The landlord with his white apron, pinned with a brass heart pin high up the sweep of his broad belly, but just under the swing of his watch-chain, rose up on his little long stool arranged behind the bar to give him judicial dignity and said: "Ho, ho, ho, getting along fine, gentlemen, any orders, gents; any old Rosicrucian like a dab of the brush? I don't touch it myself, all for peace of quietness. Ascot's a nice race meeting. Me and the Missus plan to go this year, if all goes well. We'll give you the charge of the place, and employ Alfred here as deputy commissioner of the engines, he's on the railway, ain't he? Agreed, agreed, well that's agreed. But, of course, always subject to the Missus's approval."

But how idle other people's talk seems. It would be better, I think, if speakers would first give a synopsis of what they propose to say, just as the grand old giants of the printed World of Fiction used to head their chapters. Sometimes they'd have a verse, often the most thrilling, as I have before noted, signed "Anon", most likely "Anon" standing for themselves. Even if they didn't have a verse they had a whet-your-whistle description of what was to come sometimes short.

Chapter XLIII
Love strong as death, and not less bitter.

Chapter VII
Temperament of the people, their sturdiness—The marriage rite dispensed with by the Peasantry—

State of Education—Gradual dying of Ancient Superstitions.
The Lobis-homen, or Wehr-Wolf—Its Nightly occupation—The Bruxas or Witches—Their Midnight festivals—A supper interrupted by a party of Armed Men—Courageous Conduct of a Feitor—A Dislocated wrist and Broken ribs—A vain search and a Lucky escape from Assassinators—Arrival of a Relief Party—Death of a Leader of a Marauding Gang—Burial of the Corpse by a Goatherd.

And I myself made a long time ago a short Chapter heading all ready for a Chapter, which I never wrote. It was to be for a book to be called

Under the Klinking Stars,

and that was a quotation. The Chapter was to be

Chapter Seven

Afloat—Ashore—The Saucy Glance—The Burning Pike—The Right across—The Croppy Boy—And the Moon Swam round and clear.

Now—thinking of you also I would like to give you from my store a really full-waved chapter heading, and we are in luck for I have under my hand a list of suggestions for the contents of a chapter which I will not write. But I will not waste the last so here it comes, and as you have been standing up to breast the gravelly storm as far as this without a breather, I'll call it

Chapter Two,

and here goes:

J. Toole, and Cook, and James Sullivan, and his great poster. Swede turnips, Weight-lifting, man in his walking clothes grunting. Swan song, heard record and refused to die. Vale of Aylesbury and all the falls. Waterfalls everywhere—Jem Mac. Jem Smith. The Lord Mayor's Coachman. Paintings outside booths at the Fairs. The private performance of the little play called Hand Knocks. Bob Habbijams. The M. C. Harris. Pictures on walls of Inns, and of the Lambeth School of Arms. Shapes the bus conductor. Rain. Glissade. House Boats. Walking by Seashores. Song Book Shops. The Trig of the Loup. Model Yachts. The *Moonbeam*. Names on ganzies and coaches. The Dodo Music Hall Chairman. The Little Girl who walked half a mile under five minutes. The *Ta Ta*, Midges. Man reading. The Mystery of a Hansom Cab. "Let them that built the Work Houses live in the Work Houses." By Cavern lake with candles on rafts. New York. 'mond pin in bartender's tie. Trotting horse 'res in American bar. Pictures in bars and hair- rs. Marionettes, Pompity Pompity Pomp. of Sporting heroes from Ouida. Cogers Hall. Desperate hole in grounds. Captain Webb. rford Schooners in the print. "Ah what Sceptred Race." Australian Ballads. yne Reid. Pitcairn. Bret Harte, Old ries. Hills of the Shatemuc. The es by retired Captains. Frisco, old

times. Tom Cringle's Log, and the Torch. The
Mississippi. U.S.A. Slang. Tales of the South, the
deep South. Cow Boys real and of, several, later
dates. All sorts of Newer Arabian Nights. Tom and
Jerry. Bartenders' Guides. Pirates. Facts about Wine.
Stencils. Football stories. School life. Bookplates.
Pictures in Galleries. Panoramas of Lord Mayors'
shows, and large panoramas. Dioramas. Rambles.
Biographies. Model ships for Glass cases. Who's
whos. Who's Houris? Essays and reveries. Maps.
Timetables. Ballads and Newspaper Cuttings.
Guides to Places. Price Lists. New Books of Poems.
How to make things. Old pamphlets. Three Decker
Novels. Funny Novels. Scents. Liniments. Maga-
zines. Weekly papers. Tales by old followers of
Sports. Books about old Painters. Writers like Kip-
ling. Brogues. Civilization. The Quadroon. Lady
Morgan. Bohemia. "The people I pity." Literature.
Mystery of names. Rose by any other name.
Classical Heroes and Heroines. Mills. Dime Novels.
Songs of Vagabondia. The Fancy. The Lily of
Poverty Flat. I must make pictures however they
may rowel me, as the Scotch Exiles are wounded in
the ribs by "The Lone Sheiling on a misty island".

Address Books. Press Cutting Books. First plays.
First nights. Old Plays. Pomps of yesteryear.
Jamaica. Old American River Steamers. Lions.
Irish Terriers. Irish Wolf Hounds. Old Letters.
Old Virginia. Limerick for ever. Cork, and the
Maradyke, and the live Oaks. New Orleans. The
History of the World. Souvenirs of plays. Old
illustrations. Morland the Painter. Pictures of old

sailing ships. Balzac. Dead Magazines of Art. Old
Sketch Books. Old Legends of Ireland. Plays with
brains in them as in a dish. Rebellion. Revolution.
Islands. Buried Treasure. Boat Races. Forgers.
Fighting Sailors. Mrs. Hemans. Mark Twain's Tom
Sawyer and Huck. Bad Boys' diaries. Monte Cristo.
Professional Backers. Zebras. Bonaparte's Josephine.
Mottoes, Conversation Lozenges. Old Beggars, of
course. There's no "of course" about it. At the Rag
Man's Hat. Nat Gould's Classical Racing. Seldom
is heard a discouraging word—on the Range. Valets.
One story good till another is told. The celebrated
Dan Hayes of Limerick who was the original writer
and composer of Hamlet. A Candle like a good deed
is a Naughty World beside a Canal. Practical Jokers.
Atalanta. Prophecy. Melancholy Sweet. Poetry on
Death.

Farewell to Hollywood

The last ditch is just behind me.
The last star has shot his bolt.
The last pair of lips have kissed
    Their last kiss miss.

I take my old sombrero and I go.

Comrades, Boxers boxing slow, sharing each
other's sorrows, sharing each other's joys, when
danger has threatened my darling old comrade was
there by my side. Tags of towns and family tags too.
Topers' Toasts and sentiments. Old Inns. Old
drawing-rooms, old ladies, and little old evening
parties. Not till Time his glass shall shiver. The side

Walks of New York. Sunset falling down behind the land seen from a railway carriage. Bret Harte's odour of Mignonette. California, California, the Queen of Comeallye. All sorts of places and throngs, which I have never seen. Charles Duval. Hospitality. Friendship. Humanity. The Hoodlum Band. Since the year forty-seven. John Company. York Powell. Flush Times in Alabama. Bird singing. Long nose and shiny eyes of greyhounds. Saturn. Venus. Mars. Games with buttons, with tops, hoops, kites. Aunt Sally. Hold Tight Mary. Wexford City older than Babylon. Fame again, Fred Archer. Sullivan the Irish Whispers. Old Dan. Blondin. Captain Boyton. All the Captains. How grand a day dream, a grand National Day dream. Your grand National muffler. The Bridge Jumper Fuller. Jacks for everything. Johns for honesty. Harry. Harries are often Bluff. The face at the Window. The Real McCoy. Old Devil-may-care. The Seedy Swell's song. The Shabby Genteel. Mysterious Names of old inns. Captain Davis, he who set me foresail on me mizzen-mast. Mysterious Billy Smith. Thomas Dunn English. White Tigers' Milk. Sweet Alice Ben Bolt.

And a very nice Chapter Too!

But there go my notes over my shoulder and I turn to the Good Boy and say, "Have you travelled much?" Before he replies I notice that we are strolling gently in a blue, grey, and green pleasure ground, woody, in the middle of a city. High houses all round the edges. We have, a few paces from us, pacing in time

135

to our thoughts, and they are weaving about in a Malton print, a couple, an old blade, gay but droopy. While leaning on his arm is a stately young woman still in the mind of the Eighteenth Century. There are other people in the half-light, they look a little like the Baron and Bowsie moving this way and that, but always parallel to myself and the Good Boy. From time to time they all talk a little, sometimes to each other, and sometimes to themselves. The Good Boy answers my question. He says, "Not so much as you might imagine from the peculiar look in my left eye". What is travel but an enlarging of the mind, too much enlarged the mind must snap, or wilt and perish, which is more comfortable for all concerned.

From then on we all talked
in and out of turn.

I was one time in the City of Limerick buying a horse, that's what I went there for. I had the price of a horse and every one in the City and the counties of Limerick and Clare knew well I had.

Price is all. But what of the currency?

There is a man lurking there inland among the trees. He thinks he's seen us both before on some fair green in the high lands of Europe or maybe on the prairies of the great Americas.

A fat lot he's seen if he saw me.

I'd say he was a bit of a miscreant and had acted the part in some starving troupers' band.

I am but a visitor a near pigeon or dove of passage and I saw just now in one of your main streets here in your Capital City, and Christmas approaching your Prophetic Boy and he had written on a shingle with white chalk "from Monday it will be three weeks and three days to Christmas". I saw on the pavement a gentle group of two old tattered female critics lacadaisical even in criticism. A young girl tall with straggling down curling locks of hair before her ears. In her arms inside her shawl she was holding, and he took some holding, a baby for the purpose of exciting compassion. It was a borrowed baby and the only one she could get. He had brown cheeks, curly hair and shining laughing eyes. He might have weighed three stone, and he looked like the curly haired Marx Brother. The old critics thought he looked too mature. The beggar maid had borrowed too big a babe.

You speak like a book with a bright green cover and golden clasps and mottled edges.

I have a soul. You think because I wear a pillow-case necktie and a splinter bar pin that I have not got a soul for serious contemplation. We all have it buried somewhere within. Fear of it drives some of us boys to questionable pleasures to roseate hours, to be paid for later in the disintegrating coinage of blackening silver with no tinkle to it, and on the nail, the coffin nail, a dump. I had a song I used to sing to them in damp country drawing-rooms. I sang better in a mouldering air when the wall paper was streaked with the tears of autumn storms of years gone by. All the ladies, young and old, loved to hear me. My song—hear it, my appreciating friend:

My Song

I love to think how much I love you,
I love to think how much you love
To think how much I love
To think how much you love
To love me.
There's an old dove now a crow.
I don't think the man's doing his best.

There was more, much more of it of course, but that was all the fullness of its statement. It should really be sung, I suppose, by a female voice, one of those full furry ones the poet said "like a dove's breast in the hand", and he knew what he was talking about.

I know, and then a tough guy shot himself, well shot at himself and missed. The bullet went through a ring that was in the nose of a foreign visitor and then on up through the roof without injuring the nose.

You talk out of turn and too much.

He is but an ignorant creature obtruding his noisome corrosive ideas on the fair bosom of the night.

Let him remain silent so that I may talk, and now my immediate thoughts are dissipated like old square-rigged wooden fighting ships in a gale in a picture by a marine painter in his cups.

I have even admired beauty in a man. Many a lesser girl than I has thought that the foil to beauty must be an ugly beast. Ah, a beast perhaps, but why need he be ugly? Circe's pigs—it was Circe, wasn't it, sir?—were I do not believe ugly pigs. But you don't have to worry about that. Sir, a crumbling ruin you may some day be but the clinging ivy will save you from the worst tearings and buffetings of the wild and jealous winds.

Pipe off the ivy she stands before you now or strolling alongside you, I should say, on the shelly path in and out the green coulisses of this fair scene of fitful twilight. I hate a man to be so puffed up with his idea of what the ladies love as to make himself worse than his mother dreamt of by manipulating his features into a figurehead to frighten the little fishes. I have seen a man in the city bowlegged, he couldn't help that, but he put bicycle clips on his legs and then he'd pushed his moustache up and out so that his nose looked like a turnip in a dish of bayonets—now is that fair as between us?

Don't ask me.

Well she didn't.

I don't take any notice of what they admire, I never did. When my coachman squinting along through the eight ears of the chestnuts would begin arguing with the lady on the box beside him, it'd be because she wanted him to. Perhaps she'd say the sky was green and coachee never heard of anything green but grass and he wouldn't answer her. Treat her like she was a foolish child, and she'd repeat it, and he'd say "sky's blue", and she'd say, making her voice sound like silver bells ringing inside a beaver hat, "Yes, but sometimes the sky looks green". And then my coachman gets the idea she's making a laugh of him, so he says, "Don't you tell

me them chestnuts are green. They're the same
colour as the back of my neck, when I've washed it".
Then I come up with my horn and I pushes it out
between them and gives them

> Bright rolls the Ocean,
> Also the coaches roll.

That was my business as a guard, always pouring
music on the troubled waters.

He could twirl a good horn I'm telling you, my
friend, my friend of old. He could stand up on the
back of the coach without holding on, with his stiff
chest sticking out and blowing

> Tarrah rah rah
> Tarrah rah rah
> Tarrah rah rah
> Tarrah rah

and over the hedges and far away. He laced the air
like a bird flying through the cloudy lands and
looking all the time like a cherub on a ceiling. And
I remember the time when we drank below such
cherubs. I always loved the classical, I love it still.
I sit apart and muse, and they think my thoughts
are with pattering hoofs on a dry road. What do
they know about such things? There's times I think
there's only you and me in the world, and then I
think there's only me. Then I get frightened and it
isn't a good day for the Good Boy to be frightened.
I owed it to them that named me to catch hold of

myself, so I clean my boots, I get a shine on them and out I go.

You certainly seem more charming than usual. You will not misunderstand me I know when I say I think it may be the wrapping about you of the half-light, you believe me as if I was on my oath when I say you can stand up to the fiercest sun of the most gimleting artificial light and flatten it back, and still it is the half-light which you complement best by your own half-light.

No one said ever that I was a half-light of love. I saw a case, a beautiful little case, of duelling pistols with little bullets all ready. It was to be sold by auction in this city the next day, Lot —, I forget what the number was. The auctioneer's clerk had licked the label and slammed it inside the lid of the box. He hadn't the cheek to push his label on to the butt or the barrel of a pistol. The days of duelling are over. Many days are over and every day that had a memory when it dies falls away from me from my side, from my limbs. I grow thinner, my bones will shrink after a while, but the roundness of my cheeks will go last of all and then the width of my eyes will go and puzzle—what remains?

I won't be here to see.

No, sir, you will not be here, you will have gone, melted down to grease—a cake paper.

She has you there most unkindly. The ladies they love cruelty for itself.

You did not ask me. But I know they love everything for itself. Everyone should know that.

No. No. I didn't.

Who's that fellow flittering about in the shadows remarking everything he hears? Like a mushroom born of the green grass staying close with his ear above his mother listening to her growing.

Unnatural son.

Oh he's natural enough, he belongs to shadows, pale shadows. The shadows you do see walking on the depths of a pond.

Heaven defend you, you never walked along the floor of a pond.

My sister did and when the young men, three of them, their legs twisted together and fighting one another with the surface of the water a yard above them, took her up to the air with their arms coiled about her, she said, "You moved me too soon".

Her and her sister——

Let me interrupt you, whoever you are or whatever you are, I have the honour to ask you to pause before you speak further. I have seen men in a foggy early morning biting on a bullet for less than you may be thinking of saying.

I withdraw my thought, but if I may say so, with his permission, to you, Madame, this brave blade with his pistol-butt hand tingling for the old spattered field of honour does us both less than justice. I am about to remove my hat to you, Madame, let your brave blade do the same simultaneously. Honour is satisfied, let glory wait.

You got off that ground in good time but only just. There was a look in the old eye. I have seen such before in the prime of my manhood before I sold all for the soul of music in a yard of brass.

A buyer of souls he was! Think of that!

The man's in earnest.

I have made eyes my study, the eyes of men and women and my horses. Horses' eyes tell you very little in a general way. If they have their grub and their clear water, and good straw under them, and a good stable roof over them, the looks you get from them praise God from whom all blessings flow. But when they give you that penetrating look, wide and steady, the way the man had it in the song, then the frogs of the hoof are itching for the plains and the high good lands sloping up and they are for the war break through and no revenge, or only half a break through and then revenge with tooth and heel. Some of them fight them for it. Not me, whatever way the fight goes. Them that fight them are bent for evermore.

This man speaks well. He carried himself with a style. The man who bought a soul so that he might have two.

His own and a spare.

He doesn't hear either of us luckily for he would not understand any joking now.

The spare man with the low-necked little covert coat speaks from his heart as I have done at times.

But you must not strain that ornamental object, the centre piece of the valentine. I have never expected it of you, gluttony. I have bid you farewell. His friend in front of him spoke with dignity just now in an awkward moment, that moment when the coming event of the whistling bullet sucks the air dry, to leave an alley way, to at least one heart. Extinction dignity handled well.

The dignity of the fat.

Bravery, dignity, they are always thinking about them.

Who spoke then?

The man in the shadows. Some broken-down old actor who thinks because he has squeaked and groaned and howled through a mort of parts that he has one part left, a critic weaving from niche to niche in a Valhalla.

If he was that he would be invisible.

Well he's only just visible.

They don't like being criticised.

They are right. They will stand a good deal from each other, especially as the shadows grow about them. They feel a human frailty and friendliness in the voices that come from mouths they hardly see.

Yes. The man at the back shadowed in the leaves is against them all they think because though he is only half seen all the time, still his voice is never cloudy with humanity but harsh, its own flint and its own steel.

Yes.

I love this hour of the sun's retiring. Lots of the people drink sherry at this hour, or cocktails, or perhaps make little rhymes or anything to pass away the little time. I know they always did so. It's the dissolving hour between the sunset and the night. It has always been that hour. Always where Venus holds the position on the rails, but not when the bivouac of Mars is pitched on the edge of the battle-field of blood. It is the woman pecking with her foot upon the threshold of the night.

Madame speak on.

I have no more to say.

Pardon me, Madame, discussing yourself before yourself. But was not this hour created by yourself in your long hunting with Fatima for that key of Bluebeards? She never called him Bluebeard in derision, and she never sent up her sister to watch the road for her brothers until the key was blood-stained, and found, and still you remember and you invent occupation for the hour, when your craving for the key is on you.

Some people think she is the facile Receptionist of Civilization which is only dying to rush in.

I am tired of comment. But it worries these kind creatures. It serves a purpose, it brings them together.

My old friend, the Man-Without-a-Shirt, has not spoken for a few bars, nor indeed very much. What words he said I liked.

The muscle of his throat and the sheath of the muscle of his topmost ribs are working. He will speak soon again.

I wish he would. I like to hear him.

I think, I think it to myself that these people with their loitering minds, as they go loitering up and down across the grass and between the trees, reveal themselves in their speech. But they can never speak directly to me or, in truth, I to them. I think the Good Boy and I speak the same language.

No. Ah, no. We sometimes read each other's thoughts, and if we are in a good humour we put the same words to them. But you know, and must always remember if you wish to wind about you a few worn shreds of happiness and make them glisten, that even this Good Boy will never speak the same language as yourself.

'Tis even sŏ and I agree with you that I know it, and have always known it since I left the years of discretion behind me, and left all to the advice of a licked finger held in the air.

Yes those old Sailormen's and desert Travellers' patents of the course are the cheapest in the end. In Government offices, speaking as a man of experience in them, we read only the firmament or the fire in the grate, what we did in the Summer I do not know. I joined the thick phalanx in the heel of a year, and after the breather of St. Stephen's day I did not return. Unlike those paper-hangers of other days, after raw cold mornings, I was not invalided out—I resigned. You remember those paper-hangers with their agonizing pipes puffing out on the first train, hot footed on the dawn, from Manchester to Liverpool. They were invalided out. A blacksmith smiting the morn and chasing the paper-white stars away with a pipe filled with hoof parings blasted them out of the carriage. They did not reach coma on the train. They tottered to the gravelly wayside platform, lay down, and passed into oblivion. We ought to be able to raise some sort of a conversational flash that would have that lurker in the shadows invalided out. The worst of those listening creepers is they haven't enough imagination to be horror-struck.

I have met their sort, kind Sir. I got one of them in a corner where he had a taproom table shoved up against his double-breasted waistcoat, and I with my fancy boot, kid, with a varnished golosh, pressed against the box of the table and pushed it hard against his stomach to make him attend, and yet he never flicked an eyelid at a blood curdler. The last I tried on him disgusted me with him. He didn't even take his hat off to it, not even to pass his hand across his forehead. That type of man's a clod human. Yes, human—by proxy.

I told him about my old coachee driving a team, three dead and one alive, down a hillside three miles, keeping the dead and stiffening all standing by the main strength of arm. And the one gallant leader dragging the whole blasted outfit. Those three noble-hearted animals breasted up the last bit of hill to get them on the top. With my old man whacking around and screeching, they plunged over the crest as if they were jumping a brook—and they died of it, the three great hearts burst together. But the weight of the coach and one grey leader, and him dazed, dragged and rattled them down the hillside like as if they were wooden horses in a child's toy. When they crossed a bridge in the town the dragging noise them dead horses made sounded like striking lucifer matches on a rough-cast wall. And when the old man on the box stopped there in front of the White Mitre the live one was bending at the joints and swaying propping up the dead one next him, the dead wheelers propping up one another. And coachee he bought a grass field and he put twenty

men a week digging a great hole and he buried the
three horses all strung out with the traces straight
and the coach, and he heaped in the earth on them,
and the living horse he turned out to grass for his
remaining days. And when that last horse bit his
teeth in death he buried him in his place—the off-
side leader he was. This flat face in the taproom
corner never said a "thank you" to the living or the
dead. So I gave the table one last farewell of a kick
—and that pitched his mug of beer all over his
double-breasted waistcoat and saturated his stuttering
gold watch and chain.

You did perfectly right, sir, had I been in your
place and large enough I would have done the same.

Ah! The days of yore, the days of double-breasted
waistcoats, gold watches and chains and all the paraphernalia of respect, we shall never see those days
again, they are gone. I count myself hardly past my
prime, but most everything I value has left me
standing still, or perhaps it is that those who used to
value me have not been able to pass on the faint and
fragile interest they took in me, and such as me, to
their sons and daughters, certainly not to their
daughters. I was once considered a ten-stone-four
Byron and to-day if I accept a free brief to a sub-
scription dance if I don't go ironed to my life with a
half-pound of starch rattling round in my collar, cuffs,
and shirt front and tails so long they ought to have
a knot in them, like a wild filly from the western hills.
I may shiver among the cold cigarette ends. But
why repine. I am in favour of ideas of reform and
improvement of the comforts of life. The American

fashion of moving always, when in the dusk, with a quart of hard alcohol in each hip pocket is good. Has any one among these shrubs got such?

I fear there is no happy answer to the cry of your heart.

I would, Sir, that I was in a position to walk about so armed. I believe I could so resist the temptation to guzzle alone as to wait until the eleventh hour, at anyrate, for company.

, I believe you—I thought at first you dogged me thinking I was so loaded. But I knew soon I did you an injustice. I knew soon that a man of your intelligence would never expect to find anything but a dress handkerchief and a bottle of eau de cologne on my hips.

That is life. They talk to keep themselves warm while I wore bottles once about me like cartridges in a bandolier and drained them all between sunset and sunrise, and all I drained to the toast of this hour, and I thought I was satisfied. I believe still that I was satisfied.

This flittering man on my right, Sir, talks like an actor speaking his lines to make certain that he is word perfect. But when will he appear before the public? He has had ancestors I don't doubt. It is better in these cases not to enquire too deeply. When I see some of these Gay Lotharios of the bicycle with their bagged-out trousers

Like Zouaves.

Bagged-out trousers and their bicycle clips, when —you, Sir, will forgive my talking so free—I see them reaching with their long paws through the arch trying to get hold of their tail to have something to sit on, I believe then, that Doctor Barnum was right and some of the people had monkeys for grandfathers.

Barnum my innocent is near enough. But it was another old friend of mine who thought he could place the monkey in the family portrait gallery.

Yes in the album his "Cart a Fisseek", as they said one time in Days of Old when Knights were Bold.

Old Times, we always talked of Old Times when the shadows grew long. I've seen the horses looking at their own long shadows very curious. To see a long-legged black horse twitching his ears when you twitch yours and moving along the sandy road always just ahead of you must puzzle any intelligent horse. I wish sometimes I had as much intelligence as a well-instructed horse—and no more. I can find little good any schooling I had ever did me and I tell you it was precious little I took.

This airy man behind us, Sir, speaks with a full layer of sense on what he says for all he looks as though he ate seldom. Let us turn round and comfort him, push his fat friend out of your mind, and ask him some questions.

Excuse my facing you with this young lady face to face, and asking you do you enjoy your life daily as the occupations of the hours meet you on your way?

Sir, I would say I enjoy nothing I see, hear, or feel separately, any more. I am superannuated for seeing, hearing, and feeling alone. But oh, Madame, and you, Sir, I enjoy all together seeing, hearing, feeling, at the same moment the times I once spent, the places I found myself once. But not the thoughts of my brain in the old time. I hate the thoughts I had. I put up with the ones I have now until this lady disentangled them from me with her smile.

You see I'm still a smiler.

We are all smilers here. All except that shadow man weaving to and fro, back there in about the bushes. His mouth is always down in the corners.

Madame's mouth has no corners except perhaps a kind of puss in the corners.

How well they think they know me.

That is their folly, every man must have a folly. As the lady in the play said, "If we have not a folly within us we're as good as shipwrecks wrung out and hung up to dry".

These people are worth hearing, they stumble through the thistles to the nest of the bird who laid the golden egg. When I was younger the plump ladies had golden knobs and they used to lace them with golden hairpins. Bright winkles taken from the shell on a golden hairpin straightened out, on a hard, cold, high, dark morning of a bank holiday, was considered to place a man among the immortals. I left him to it when I gathered my horses in my hand, and with the long charabanc behind us we slipped down into the brown velvet shelter of the stable yard. And when I had my horses in the stalls I'd go into the yard bar and rest my head against the whitewashed wall beside the chimney-piece while they prepared for me the milk and rum hot, and while I waited I slept and I dreamt. But I have forgotten what I dreamt.

You should never forget a dream, they are always so perilously near the edge of the crater. "The unfortunate crature," as the wit couldn't help himself saying, "he's always on the edge of something." But watch the lady, she will make an oblique remark to Bowsie, sliding it off the Man-Without-a-Shirt. Her lips move, they are curved like cupid's bow permanently. I bet you she's got a tongue like an asp. Not at all, I was wrong, it' like a short sword in the short ribs.

Sir, if you can hear me for the noise of the wind which makes an Æolian harp of your ribs. Do you believe your friend has a voice? If so nudge him and perhaps he'll take his head out of his chest and give us a song low and sweet, a murmuration of a fo'c'sle drone. My tall and gallant friend here would like to hear something of the days that are no more. He says I am of all times and none at all.

See she swings her old blade round on her arm to face the music.

And Bowsie stands forth with his Lieutenant behind him.

> If I could think of a story O,
> Oh bubbleyum billorio,
> If I could think of a story O
> I'd wipe the blood from my sleeve.
> My friend he died in a crooked ditch
> High on the old mountains O.
> But ere he died

Upon his side
He placed my sleeve
To slither it O
With his fresh blood
So red and grand.
And his last words to me
Were these that I can ne'er forget O.

Eighteen years my age,
A maiden loves me.
In a red bog hole
I die my death,
I die for a notion O.
But my blood shall never dry
While my story holds its sway
And so it will with you remain
Until you join me,
Or find a sadder story,
To take away
From mine the sway.

I have heard no sadder story, the laugh is out of me.

Lend me your handkerchief, Squire.

Tell me, innocent, do you weep for his maiden's love, or for his blood so saturating the sleeve of his friend? But no, don't tell me.

I will not tell you.

Of course she is right. Do you want, old fool Squire, to steal her secret from her?

Hail to old Flitter the Ditch among the bushes. I thought we'd cold-shouldered him for keeps.

You will never suppress him. He requires no ordinary sustenance. He lives on the same diet as that classic hero—there was a horse called after him —but such a lot of horses have been called after classical heroes. Ah—I have him—Chittabob, "and his name is Chittabob".

Who first made that phrase "the best horse that ever looked through a bridle"?

Who indeed? Who made all the best phrases? The ones you won't find in a dictionary of quotations. Some day you and I and your friend Mr. Bowsie and the bare-breasted Baron must put our memories together and bring the buckets up out of the Well.

Yes, Sir, and who first put the name of Star Gazer on a horse?

Baron, you should know better than any of us, better even than the tall blade with the lady leaning on his hilt.

Ah, my shining boy, if I ever knew I would have forgotten by now. If you call me a blade you must call me a rusty old blade.

Not so rusty, "not so dusty", pop comes another phrase not rusty, and clear enough to illuminate a moonless night, a prime sword.

May the lady who leans on the hilt—

I think the leaning was from the hilt to the lady.

No, and no, no, never. May I ask the Baron, and I ask because I can imagine my own feelings perched up in the circumstance about which I ask. Baron, you have known single Star Gazers. Did you ever stand up and blow your horn out of a happy heart while you knew the coach was drawn by a team of Star Gazers?

Watching the transit of Mars pursued by the mincing feet of Venus.

Mister Bowsie, it's a pleasure to hear you.

Did you, Baron, ever see together four Star Gazers?

Watching the transit of Jehu.

Madame, you will please excuse our beefy friend. He, it is easy to see, never saw a star in his stirabout.

Who said that at first?

Madame, I never saw such a team. And I do believe had I been behind such I would not have remained on this terrestrial globe long enough to recall them. Unless the name of the coach was "Impunity"—that's a good word!

It took a bit of doing, Baron.

There were several "Vivids" and "Rockets" and a "Meteor".

Now he's off on the Road. That's a good term "the Road", and it had its full meaning, I suppose, for only a few years, and it is rough and ready justice in honour, that it was the Son of Adam who made the road possible.

First, as they told me when I first felt ribbons in my fingers, were the long muddy troughs running through the land. Then, in a moment, the metalled roads of MacAdam. Then the spinning wheels sang everywhere. They passed through villages and passed isolated cottages and everywhere they cheered the hearts of the women, and little boys and girls, and anything that will cheer the hearts of these little ones cheers mine—because I can't help it. The men on the box. Three men on the box, my grandfather, my father, myself, saw the green ribbons of the grass on either side of the road and they saw looking up above it the round bright cheeks of children happy to see us rattle along. Just a short few years and the Road was over. Not three generations for it was new in my grandfather's days and sunk at the end of mine. And what sunk it was in the mind of another Scot—Stephenson—and his engines and his railways. There was a mighty pumping up of Romance on the Railways, I remember.

The Railway Library. Exciting! Oh, very exciting! Stories in paper covers at a shilling a shake. Clawing hands that came through railway carriage windows at night and throttled sleeping commercial travellers in black satin waistcoats and strange howls outside in the tunnel. The banshee of the railways. To come on a tunnel in the middle of the side of a withered grass hill was enough to make a moderately stout heart quail. Very few of the young boys of my youth would have, if alone, cared to shout into the mouth of a tunnel

"Come out".

Tunnels had a dismal smell, the same as the smell down below in the first Madame Tussaud's.

I don't want to get the Big Clanging Bell and shake your nerves. I believe you all are shaky in the nerves like the idle rich.

156

Hark to Flitter-Down-the-Vistas. And why a bell? Why the Hell bell?

Because it is long past the hour of the closing of this Midway Pleasance and I must do my duty.

Haven't you been doing it all the time by coming the Old Schollar on us?

My duty and lock the gates and I don't believe any of you except perhaps the lady are capable of climbing the high railings. And though it's as fine a summer night as ever I saw it will take time in passing.

Pardon me, Big Chief, was it you that called me "beefy"? But in my younger days, yesterday, or the day before, I having eaten one bread page of my sandwich and the leaf of ham, used the last bread leaf to make into a soft mould by working it between my fingers, and with my knife, on a seat, using a little water filched from under the bills of the ducks in the lake. And then, with the mould palmed, I engaged you in conversation, borrowed your key to look through the wards and see if I could see Constantinople and its minarets reflected in the Bosphorus, as I told you some one said was possible, and placing the key behind my back for an instant of time I took an intaglio of its make-up. You remember a handsome man with a red beard and deer-like eyes who failed to find Constantinople in the cracks of a key. Ere the light had come to enclose that day a replica of your key was cooling itself inside the fender of the sitting-room of my apartment on the south side.

Why is he not in uniform if he's a keeper?

I am a plain-clothes keeper and I bid you all a pleasant good night. I have enjoyed your conversation, especially from the lady, and I trust you have not found my occasional appearances restraining on the freedom of your accents wild. I have wished to be as little a keeper as may be. But, even in mufti, the desire to ring the closing bell on other people's jollity is never entirely absent from the keeper's heart. I give you five fond farewells.

Goodbye.

Goodbye now.

Slán leat.

Adieu.

Au revoir.

Dream softly.

And you also.

He turns in early. The first one up in the morning gets the biggest mushrooms.

He showed, to me, a loathness to depart.

There are few men who, past their prime, can stand up awake and unashamed of themselves before a Summer night. We have here four brave such, and one far fairer, and far braver. The lady in this case. And with a poet in his Autumn, and in my late Summer, I discussed the best sorts of conversation, and I was all against the presence of the fair ones except for the duet.

The Jew and the Jewett.

He will have his jokes. He polished them out of the rough metal in the old mossy days when he wore down the hearth-rug in the Civil Service of the tax-payer. Gazing through his office window at the wild

energetic play of the younger sort who abandon
the perambulators containing their admiring sisters,
or brothers, three to a pram and more coming, they
should build two-decker prams, to throw themselves
into the nourishing joys of two twirls and a kick, or
the blithely swinging of a battered camán.

My poet was with me in so far that he believed
good conversation was impossible in a group of
several men and women. But his ideal was one woman
and four men. I suppose we seek to shine, and the
song receipt said—

Take a pair of sparkling eyes.

Mine don't sparkle. Don't tell me they do—they
dream.

Sparkling or dreaming we must please them or
collapse. Therefore I say this moment is propitious.
The number's right. Let us be at our ease sitting in
a half-moon on these chairs. They are marked "two-
pence each" but to us they are free. Lend a hand,
boys. Mister Bowsie, do not try to carry two at a
time, they will only entangle you.

Ah yes, I see, thoughtful one, two for the senior,
one for himself and one for his legs, a pity those old
legs should ever die.

The crunching of the gravel, the dragging of the
chairs, so pass away the lives of mortal men. We
illustrate it in one summer's night.

I remember in my youth a song—

"One Summer's Night in Munich."

It went through the English-speaking world and to the far Colonies of the British Empire like a rocket. I started on the strength of it to walk all the way from Paris there. I was carried forward by my romantic idea of a city of old gabled houses, bright dancing, and beer in decorated beer mugs. But men paced that road because of some magic in the word Munich.

People have had the key of a park before and have sat on chairs within it and talked on a summer night before this, far away and long ago. But we are five such as have never sat together before. If the mufti garden keeper had stayed he would have spoilt the set. But we are ourselves alone, and in conglomeration, unique. Let us talk, about what? About politics? Dished. About ourselves? Yes, about ourselves.

Truth or a fancy tale?

From yourself first and it will be truth I know, because though you could act one you could not tell a falsehood.

Silence for the lady.

Forgive me not rising to bow for you. But this young man has fixed my legs so fairly on the extra twopence-worth that before I could straighten them and get upon my feet your true tale would be under way. I take off my hat to you and kiss my hand.

I was on a good thing once but missed it. I was an understudy for Miss FFoillett and the woman, whoever the hell she was, took sick at six o'clock of a November evening and I did no more than know an odd word of the part. And that night we had a raw

Willie Reilly. He came off the train running. It was delayed with a broken coupling—broken coupling is the word. Willie Reilly had read his part and washed it out of his mind again with porter and the hard stuff on the road. He was the loveliest Willie Reilly ever trod those staves. The band was good. The people were grand. I don't know what he told me in the play. I don't know what I told him. I had the cues and no more. But he told me that he loved me. And now, gentlemen, I'm saying it to you, he never became my lover.

We came out on the street after the curtain was down, and I said to him, "Did you eat anything? With all that drink you ought to have eaten". He said no but he was all right. "Why should I eat," he said, "it'd be a waste." But I said that I had some money and we should have some prawns or maybe cockles, and he took some and a little more porter, and "Ah", he said, "it is a waste, I'm going across the bridge," he said, "to one of them hotels along the quays and to-morrow I'll buy you a ring, my girl. If there is going to be to-morrow."

"That's queer talk," I said, "from a Willie Reilly." "There's many kinds of Willie Reilly," he did say to me. "And now take a hop, skip and a jump for your home, for I must study on a part where there's only one cue and it's one every one knows."

"What's that one?" I say.

"A secret, my girl," he says, and then he takes off his hat, shakes his head about in the night and foots it away.

I'd only gone a little way along the road when I thought to myself I'll turn round and look along the bridge and I'll see my sweetheart walking there where the lamplight falls. And I looked back, but he was not there, and while I was looking two or three men, old men tottering in their steps, were running to the quay wall and loosing a rope that was holding a boat, and I ran up to see what it was all about, and toward the sea I looked, and there was Willie Reilly's face above the water for a minute—and then it was gone. And the rotten old boat with the two old cripples going out to the place where he sank and looking into the water and crying out loud. Ah, but what else could they do, the poor old men!

When they came back I gave them half a crown. I said, "You're cold, old men, get yourselves a hot drink in the place called 'The Happy Brig'—wasn't it a wonder I remembered the name of it and me never in it in my long life? Indeed it wasn't a very long life I had passed me up to then. No one ever saw the body of that young man again. I would be happy now if I saw one bone of his little finger.

She speaks the truth. She always had the habit of it. So help me, God, I would sooner be the body of that young man a tossing always in the middle deeps of the sea, and that young woman to think so well of me, than to be as I am, greasy, fat, unlovely and unlovable, no one to care whether I am carried out on a tide or buried with musical honours, and three times three and a tiger, and the estate of my body paying for all. I think always back to myself, the decrepit old egotist.

Don't say that now. You have friends here and as many friends anywhere as any man ever had.

Yes, I have friends, I am thankful for them, I like them well, as well as I am able to like any one. And they like me as well as they can like any of their friends. So, so, I talk too much.

Not a word too much. But you weary yourself with your round and round thinking. I knew a pony skew bald, bought from a circus he was, and every now and then, in the middle of a crossroads, on any wide space, something would make him think of the days of his youth, and he would run round and round in an imaginary circus ring. Come now, Baron, you heave up something out of the days of yore, out of your own career and of the times which were about it.

I remember on a certain night, many many years ago, I was trim as a bridegroom—that's Shakspere! Sleeping a beauty sleep, for I had not long pulled the eiderdown over me in the cosy bedroom of my delightful apartments. I was lodged at the time (I was in funds, I had come right away from the pebbly beach) close to the Court of St. James. I do not know how long my eyelids had been closed for I had not got my watch at the time and my landlady hated clocks about the place. It was her say, poor soul, they were furnished lodgings, she was born in the Dials, married in St. Giles, and buried her sporting whitesmith in Shoreditch. "And by this and by that," she'd say, "I'll die in St. James." She was illiterate, almost completely illiterate, and I think her hatred of clocks came from the fact that she could only read them at the hour, and perhaps, by good luck, at the half-hour. And because she could not read their thoughts she hated their flat white faces. I think that was the trouble, it looked at her while she smelt my bay rum and wondered was it poisonous, or was it like the grand old encourager of the timid heart with the sailor label on the bottle.

I awoke suddenly. Always a light sleeper to this day, even under a hedge, for I have studied in that college, but that is neither here nor there and depends entirely on the season of the year. I awoke suddenly as I knew by the "crinkles of my nose"— Shakspere again!—that there was somebody in the room standing up high like a cliff by my bedside. Well, it was all hands to the pumps: some one must say something, so I said, "Strike a light. There's matches and a candle here by my bedside. On guard and God defend the right." I gently closed my eyes, I hate a sudden light on them, and when I opened them again the candle was burning up straight—and tall and upright on his pins, standing by my bedside, was a tall, stiff-built, toff-like bloke with a long face and a false moustache, but thin hair on his crown. He was wearing a kind of old mustardy coloured suit, a bit fridgy at the edges and he didn't say a word, not at first.

He took a large black handkerchief from his inside breast pocket, he dropped it over my revolver which was lying on the little table by my bedside, he wrapt it up in the black handkerchief, then he blew on the bundle, then he opened the bundle and, hey presto! cockolorum jig, the revolver was gone!

"How now?" I said. I was irritated.

He turned the black handkerchief round, made a little ball of it, blew it another kiss, opened it out and there was an egg in it. Then he spoke in a refined voice, I'd say from across the river. He said, "How do you like your eggs, soft or hard-boiled?" I said, "Hard". So he whacked the egg down on the floor and by the noise it made I knew it was one of those china nest-eggs. I was sorry afterwards I didn't say "soft". I wonder what he would have done if I had. I said, "A conjurer?" He said, "No, a highwayman and a burglar", and he began walking towards the door. I said, "Shut the hall door as you go out, I'm the only poor little coon in the house, the landlady is gone on the boat to the seaside for a couple of days, the floor below this is occupied by a firm of solicitors, and the street floor is a hairdresser's; you might find some material there to wax your moustaches." I'd noticed they were very poor and woolly. All the time I was speaking he was standing on one leg very polite, and then he shut my door after him and went away quietly and I only *just* heard him pull the front door to. He was gone. I blew out the candle.

I don't know how long after that it was, my room was very tucked into itself with shutters over the window and thick curtains over the shutters, but once again I got the sensation that there was some one standing by the bed. I said again, "It's either you back again or your mate, but whichever you are, please don't spare me, strike a light". Well, the match came on and the candle-flare flared up again and there was my nocturnal surpriser back again.

Poor shrimp, he looked lost! I noticed he'd got a new coat on over his old one, very roomy, built for a heavyweight, evening coat, very old-fashioned. I said to him, "How now, Blue Eyes?" I'd noticed them probably for the first time, blue they were, pale. He said, "Lead me to your treasure chest". "All right," I said, "but I'll have to put on my dressing-gown, getting suddenly up out of a warm bed like this". "Here you are, old toff," he said, taking the dressing-gown off the back of the chair where it was lying and holding it up until I got out of the bed. Then he helped me into it, handing me my slippers which were close by the chair. So we started up to the attic where I had permission to store some of my oddments, including a box with nails in it. The box was locked, but I had had the forethought to bring my bunch of keys with me, so I opened it and we both looked in. There lying reclining, you might say, on a sort of a bed of newspapers, was a group of waxen fruit and flowers. It had belonged to some of the old people. I told the highwayman I was intending to take them to a meeting of our Antiquarian Society to-morrow night "just for a show down", or words to that effect, so I could not care to be parted from them. He said, "Close the lid, it'll soon be morning", so I closed the chest, locked it and stood up facing him and said, "You are wearing evening dress". He said, "Naturally, it is evening". "In that case," I said, "reach into the tail pocket and give me back my revolver." He said, handing over the weapon, "It don't work". "Who would?" I said. "You," he replied, "are a philosopher." "No," I said, "an actor." He said, "I wish I'd known that earlier in the night, I could have put you into a very good part. Kindly show me out". So I took him down to the hall and I bolted the door after him.

You did perfectly right, the man was obviously behaving in a way unaccustomed to the clothes he wore. He was a masquerader. If you had a sword in your hand and struck it through him and wiped it on a clean linen you would not have got the true stain of blood but something like dissolved pasteboard. There have been in the past, and perhaps even more so to-day, though I am out of the ring and know nothing about it, far too many of these pasteboard knights, these gaslight swells. Objects of derision who pretend to be walking battleaxes. I wish my grandfather was alive and with us here to-night for he could tell us what they were like in his days. Such creatures as these always start from somewhere and the place and hour of their first appearance is ascertainable somewhere, some time. They are not fundamental creatures like the hyena and the zebra hailing from far away and the misty past of our green isle. Though I cannot swear that we ever had the hyena or the zebra in our woodlands and drinking from our streams.

These Solomon Lobbs, these ploughmen bold, these ranting cavaliers came among the people later on. They invented themselves, and when they stept from the dressing-tent into the arena, their band, their fellowship, and their camp followers began to worry such as my friend the Baron and us all with their guttering candles of romantic nothings, a candle wrongly placed can spoil the slant of the bold-faced sun.

Reality is the food of life. Experience realized brings wisdom up to the top of his strength high and clear of all. The horse who hits the rail in the first fence and is still standing takes no more risks but rises over all the rest like a free bird, and I wish us all, even the oldest of us, for it is never too late to jump large, no worse fate than to be a learnéd bird master of his earthly flight.

I lie on my stomach in the grass and I see heroes flying over forest fences, at your word, sir, you conjure them up before my eyes. You must be strangely gifted.

All men are strangely gifted.

You've said it. We know it now, but everybody in the noisome world don't know, and let us not tell them. Let us think we are, and so be, free of all bodily aches or fear of aches like the Nonebodies, the will-o'-the-wisps, the spirit nimbos, just floating along in the air, our shoe toes just clearing the flowers of the bog lands, singing every man his own song. I was a two-sworded knight, a warrior grand, chasing my way through warriors, all my equals, and going from one bellying cloud to another by milky bridges a hundred miles up in the sky. One false step I'm off the bridge, another true step and I'm back again, and the poor stone-picking grovellers down on the surface of the earth below me didn't know that they were so near to having a twelve-stone warrior coming down on them like a bullet from aloft. You'd be surprised to see how the horses who ride up there do adjust their stepping to the yielding swellings of the clouds, just a glancing step on off, off on. So there is no time to sink into the white bundles of vapour. Most every one who travels in an aeroplane complains that the bird's-eye view of the earth becomes a bore. But we don't have to put up with that, we can adjust the reflections in the mirror behind our eyes and with a touch of the finger of the mind adjust all the angulated mirrors between us and the ground. And so we can see everything that goes on down below us as though we stood upon the soil ourselves. The adaptable mind has great and most acceptable powers. The mind is, that is with us, adapting and adaptable all the time the two powers blent together like one pulse. If I could make new right words to tell you how we hit the trail every instant you would look at me and not see this gross and shadowy bulk of butcher's meat. You would see me as good to see as the Good Boy, and he doesn't blush when I speak so of him, why should he—being the well-beloved is nothing to be ashamed of.

You tell me what I know was true once, as true as pen and ink or printer's ink, and now it is true but not in ink.

I could perhaps get myself up with the help of a tailor with brains to look something like you, perhaps even in this moon shadow to deceive any ragamuffin missing his last bus and squinting through the railings. That is if we were nearer the edge of this green park. Where we are we are entirely ringed about with green trees. I could imagine myself, if my imagination answered well to my wish, a second Good Boy, but it were better that I imagined myself an improvement on myself—one of Myselves. But among the several I am dizzied.

There is one of us here. The Man-Without-a-Shirt—he lets me call him so.

It was a baronial shirt?

He never allows the imaginary personage that he is dizzy him.

If I wind my little head too much one way, I wind it back again the other way just enough and no more to leave my head a rocking as it goes, not dizzy. I was sitting just now, in a good seat two rows behind the band, seeing a turn in a Variety Show—very grand drop scene—a palace with pillars, and just inside the proscenium arch curtain, very heavy wine red with gold ropes and tassels. And there was a small quiet man in a clown's dress, very quiet, just some black and red dots running here and there and a clown's hat very peaked, and he had a hat cord very long, that was so every time the hat fell off him he could pull it back to him and put it on. This man never spoke a word. But an attendant in white satin court clothes carried in a white board with a gold frame and on the board was written "Dondooit" or "Dooditto"—I forget which—"will positively attempt to walk the cord".

Dondooit then began to hurry about the stage from one side to the other, then more slowly and I could see that he was measuring it by pacing. Presently he was satisfied. He went towards the wings first to his right, then to his left, and each time he signalled by clasping his hands together. Three stage hands in their own old clothes, or maybe overalls, came in from either side and began fixing the upright for each end of the tight-rope or cord or wire or whatever it was to be. The arrangements were all looked over very seriously by Dondooit, every bolt tested and every strain. Then he came down to the conductor and looked at him very fixedly, and the conductor took from his waistcoat pocket a small tin whistle and handed it to Dondooit, who put it to his lips, pursing them up very prettily, and blew a thin silver note: it went all through the theatre into every corner of it. As soon as the note had died away the court-dressed attendant came on carrying a snood of thin cord on his arm. Dondooit took the cord from him, and with a great deal of fussing and trouble, and smacking of clumsy interfering fingers, the cord was fixed between the two uprights and stretched across the stage about five feet from the ground. Then Dondooit having carefully wiped the whistle returned it to the conductor. The stage hands, after some signalling into the wings, came on with a beautiful little step-ladder covered in green velvet. This was placed at one end of the rope. Dondooit took off his hat and using it as a balancing assistance went on the stage through the exercises of a man about to walk a tight-rope or a slack wire. Then he took hold of one of the stretchers or grips which governed the tightness of the cord and pulled on it. Result—the cord snapped in the middle and the ends flew out, one of them appeared to hit Dondooit on the chest, but he made light of it, it was nothing compared to the catastrophe of the broken cord. He stood there close to the footlight facing the audience in the ruins of his act. A tall, stately lady, with magnificently large furs, and a tight red wig, and a long green earring, who had entered the omnibus-box unobserved by the Baron, stood up, threw back the furs from her magnificent corsage, and revealed a pair of very large but shapely lily-white arms glistening with slave bracelets. She slid off one from each arm, one heavy gold set with sapphires, the other heavy gold set with emeralds, and she tossed them on to the stage and they fell close by the side of the failed rope-walker. He removed his hat and bowed to the lady. Then turned back to the broken cord. He loosed either end from the uprights and knotted the broken ends together, removed the whole cord from the machine and laid it out across the stage.

About this time I noticed that the bracelets were gently moving along the stage, one behind each other, towards the box where the gorgeous lady was still residing. Dondooit again using his hat as a balancer approached one end of the cord as it lay on the ground. But he appeared to pause in his mind and then he turned away from the cord and went up the stage and off. Presently he returned with the manager, I suppose, very fine large man in evening dress; this large man shook his head and went away. Dondooit turned woebegone sad eyes towards us as though seeking our compassion. And then as he lowered them he noticed the moving bracelets. With him in such a case it appeared that thought and action were as one leaping on each other's back. He darted on to the wings. He darted back; he had a spike with him and a mallet, and he was in time; it was a race and a scramble, but he pinned the second bracelet, the emerald one, to the stage. The other one was already going up on its black thread to the voluminous grand lady in the box.

Removing his hat the great little Dondooit placed the bracelet neatly, like a small coronet, on his skull top and put his hat on again over it. He walked into the wings. He returned and stood with his arms folded in a Napoleonic attitude while the stage hands removed the tight cord joint. And the white court card came in again and slowly passed across the stage with the white notice-board in a golden frame and the words were "Dondooit" (yes, that's the right name) "will positively attempt to jump through a white balloon from the height of forty feet".

I didn't wait to see him try to do it, I would if I could, but I had an appointment across the whole city. That's the way it is, I wish I didn't have any appointments at all. In my tawny youth I did have appointments but I didn't bother about them, neither did the party at the other end of the engagements. Mutual dishevelment of the orthodox. And now because we are under the stars and the night is young all them things is unravelled, so what about it, say I?

You talk like a man who had much experience in using words without a thought to the ingredients which made those words.

I heard a clergyman once preaching and his voice,

173

and the inflections of it, kept me with my bright ears forward and cocked. He must have thought in his youth in terms of elocution and in its particular values. He was preaching of Joseph and his brethren and how each of the brothers found his money in his sack. But at the word "sack" he set his mouth, I suppose, into a narrow slit of hate, for the word came through his lips with disgust and an anger that would bundle away all sacks for ever. I know he had no love at all for the word. In his mind about it clung the picture of a dead thing in a sack, a filthy sack lying on a slobland, or a sack half filled with mouldy yellow meal. "Sack"—horrible sack! He was a man who lived in the particular word and not in the general flow of words, perhaps the word "flow" there as it comes from my lips would have brought to his mind another sack—"what a lot of sack and so little bread". I would to God this minute I could, and so I could if all your wills will help me, take away from half the words I remember their bitter ungenerous meanings and give them their sweet memories only. How lovely that would be! Excuse me, friends, if here I unfold the clean cambric handkerchief from my breast-pocket and with it wipe the shining globule of a venerable tear, the first in many years, from the corner of my left and winkless eye. I have often longed to weep the full rolling tears of happiness but experience of long ago has taught me that tears can be only enjoyed alone, perhaps on a mild day with a south-westerly wind, on an iceberg under the indigo vault of a faultless sky. Tears wrung out in company, four eyes weeping all together, become an embarrassment to each other irrespective of ownership. And who shall first cry "halt, enough!" becomes the angry thought behind the last defence of each brain. A few diminuating sniffs and the instant is closed for ever. Farewell, farewell to tears! No, no, never say "farewell for ever", that is the lazy man's dodge. Getting near the end of his rope he believes he can make himself safe by cutting off that end. The first joke you remember and the end —if you could cut off the end—of the rope, so that it had no end left. The best thing you could do with it would be to bury it, and taking a piece of perishable wood write on it, with an indelible pencil, "Here lies the rope's end, therefore the rope itself has no end and is immortal". Could you bear with me I would people a cemetery with remembrances as clear as that. But I have other thoughts in my round head. I live for life as we all do, and not for the lugubrious pleasantries of obituary opportunity. If I had a musical instrument, and could play it, I would accompany myself to a song which I would sing, if I could sing. But all I can do is to toss the round back of my hand to you each, beginning with the lady who waves herself about before me, and blow a kiss to each of you, and suggest by an oblique glance from my good eye to the Good Boy, that he should tell us why they love him so.

I want to tell you that. I have for a while now wanted to explain this loving fact to myself, and yourselves. But I cannot do it properly to my own satisfaction. Anyway what of it—they love me, I believe, because I love myself, not as my particular self but as a man of better luck than discretion, a man who realizes that there is such a thing as living without fear.

What a hope! I hope it. I hope it may be possible, and I have always played a part as if I had discovered the secret of throwing away the tangling cloak of fear from my shoulders and from about my ankles. So those who love fear and hug their love love me because they think I am no competitor. Perhaps for two or three strides along an open wide road with a good sky over me or for perhaps a few cracks across a city pavement and an inch or two of the gay hard stuff in my little round stomach, I have been without fear. But still I try to put on my appearance, the appearance of fearlessness. There are others who have different reasons for loving me. They love me because they think I represent an essence, the essence of a cheerful heart unmixed. That makes them satisfied with themselves because it makes them feel more valuable than me because more complicated, a blend of many essences. "About their love," as the song says, "I don't complain." But I hold it of little value, and it will stand to me as a poor passport. I would like best to think of the love of little children and small animals who perhaps fear me no more than they fear a chuckling little shallow stream running over chaneys. And to myself I believe such a stream gave me my first three-sensed joyfulness. The sound of the rippling stream, the sight of the shining chaney, and the smell of bright spring water cleaving its way through the flowery smells of the morning. I was put together

for the day so easily then, a pushing into the smallest
of small clothes, a pulling little arms into little sleeves,
a stuffing in of tiny shirt tails, and I hit the day. And
I'm telling you no lie I expected the day to be grand
in its heart to see me. And that is why they love me,
the best of them, because I expect them to be glad
to see me and to even think of me.

Our chested friend. Oh, forgive my personal note
upon your appearance, my friend. In this bluey light
strange tricks get played with our forms and while
I am, without manners, pointing at you, perhaps the
depth of the scene has taken a pleasure in reeling
back my forehead, so much admired by my dear
mother long ago, and bringing forward into white
light my nose. So I am a ship in a dark ocean, my
nose the figure-head, my mustachios bobstays, my
little artist brush the dolphin. The nautical terms ever
charmed me—this lady is always to me a three-
decker meeting a golden ocean dawn.

You're a charmer.

Our chested friend never asked me what I was
loved for. Because he knows I was never loved more
than a little and never for very long. I was loved for
a moment in profile because I seemed set so to stand
away for the scene. That is why my mother loved
me, after the ordinary, fair enough, mother's love
had got so weak in its little pat-pat-patter of the
heart that something more was required. And then
she saw me standing like a cardboard figure, stout
cardboard, against the foolish round setting of a
street or a garden. The fact that I was a flat figure of
a man was all the way to her heart for me. She

thought only she could see me from where she stood, others would see me edge on and so nothing but a line, or others opposite her would only see me on the unpainted side of my stout cardboard. In a lesser way other women not my mother have looked at me in the same way but without that faint trace of the maternal which she had by right and not by taking thought of another good trait to own.

They love me, those that do, if they do love me, because I look as if I were going to produce an old-timer's tip out of a wide pocket. They forget for a moment my nickname, the Man-Without-a-Shirt. They never believed me that I preferred to have my bosom free. They said "Impecuniosity", and many of my friends could not spell it, especially, as you say, on a Saturday afternoon. The real ones, the ones I valued when I lived in the same world as them and breathed the same air, they loved me because they believed I had never worked. They, like most of us, believed that because man did eat an apple he must never eat again only when he had earned his grub in the sweat of his brow. But I believed that sweat had been wiped away in a sweat of the greatest blood that ever flowed. They were the old dogs that cannot learn new tricks, and they believed, if it were possible, that I had unlearned their old tricks—and so in me they thought they had a chance of loving a brimmer to the full. Perhaps they were right, perhaps they were wrong. I will not tell you. Men call me "Baron" and the "Man-Without-a-Shirt". But I call them by no names but "Woman", "Man" or "Child", and always "friend" for that goes for all. The friend here before me who was first asked why he was beloved said his friends thought he was without fear. I am sure they did. My friends never thought of me in connection with fear at all. I was like Fata Morgana to them, but she was a great mare, and when I was young some that carried her blood in them were shaking the sod to a far faster tune than

Tantivy, tantivy, tantivy.

None of you asked me in words to tell you why I was beloved. But that didn't stop me telling you a thing you did not believe possible, a thing you didn't want to know but a thing you are now very glad to know.

This man, this friend with us and about us has made himself cause and effect, perfectly clear to me, at least all was clear while he spoke, but I am not so certain now. I am of course a little older, a few minutes older, than I was. In this air of a summer's night minutes expand and contract under their own propulsion. And how is that though the stars and the moon are only sloping gently on their studied tracks, and taking part in no dance, still the shadows seem to drift this way and that and the Baron, who was in the shining light, is now folded in a shadow.

I come out again from my shadow to ask you to say truly why you are loved by your friends.

If I must answer such a question truly I must imagine that it is true that my friends love me. Well, speaking out of the folds of the wrapping of my imagination, this old parcel speaks: I am loved by my friends because it is easier for them to love than to hate. They are able to love all together to the same tune. Hate of me would be more trouble, it would have to be forced up by energy, personal and particular. Community Hate stops when the switch is off. People loved me because they were glad to think they would never be asked to take my place. They loved to think that I filled the whole of it so fully that there was only room for me there. This, it seems to me, is the exact opposite of the reason for the love of the Man-Without-a-Shirt. My friends don't even love me because they think I love them, they feel happier for not thinking so. They love to think that there is a deep and chilly moat full to the brim, dark as night, or bright as steel, always between their wisdom and my folly. They believe that always in the end they will have the laugh at me, or anyway that it will be so that they ought to have the laugh and that they believe, well, they think, is the same thing. But what does it matter as long as they love me?

He always says truth in his last words. Let us hope it will be true with him always and with the last words of all, and with us all. You have been so delicate that you, not one of you, have asked me to explain why I have been beloved. You thought the answer too easy. You would have, being still able to speak without choking, said I was loved because to look was to long. But you would have been wrong. Simple enough and you know it, you know that longing is not love. I was loved because I never loved myself, because I was never, as they say, in love with love, because I never gave love a thought, because I never hated, that is why I am loved.

I remember one summer night, not very different in some ways from this one, I opened the window of my room because the sun of the day had made the walls hot and the place stuffy. I looked out into the night and my lamp which was burning brightly shone a ray across the narrow street straight into a tree that grew in a churchyard, and the light must have shone on the closed eye of a sleeping blackbird and startled him awake, for he straightened his throat and sang, sang for me alone. In the whole of that city, perhaps in the whole world, I was the only man, and me little better than a post-horn-blowing fool, who had a blackbird singing in answer to his lamp. If a myriad things can happen at the same moment on earth then a myriad breaths of earth can be taken together and only one thing happen. I thought while he sang I and my bird were the centre of a great cool world. I was so happy in my innocence that I did not know then that some parts of the earth were blistering that moment under the hot sun. When it was night in my street I thought it was night everywhere. On that thought I moved my lamp and my blackbird fell into sleep once more.

Ah, sir, the whizzing of the earth on its plane set by God stopt for you and your shining bird in that moment, and I believe it and I'll set my stubby crooked teeth into that and I'll believe it until I die.

It makes a picture to me, the Baron leaning out of his window and the blackbird, 'tis black as a sloe, the blackest thing in sight always. As far as I can think a blackbird is blacker than every one about him in colour. I have seen him perched on a bough over a clergyman and with mourners in a church-yard. I suppose, Baron, there were no mourners in your graveyard in that night time.

Not as I observed.

Well, even against the mourners all in black I saw a blackbird grey them. And a blackbird has a cheerful song, not so cheerful perhaps, but full of courage and that's the best of all. God give us all bravery, well the look of it and the sound of it. I wonder what picture came to the eyes of all of ye when you heard the Baron talking. It depends, perhaps, on what pictures you were brought up on. And I don't mean flittering pictures on the screen, but the pictures in frames hanging on walls. What pictures did you first see the light through, Baron Bold?

The first picture I remember was of a church and a churchyard in snow time, it had a red sky. The windows were lit up and I thought to myself if the snow's as deep as that the people wouldn't be able to get out and go home until they were dug out. "Snowplough," I said to myself, though at the time I'd never seen one. I was a very intelligent child. I wonder now I didn't get over-heated in the brain. Perhaps I did and they never noticed it. I think when I grew to manhood the noise of wheels on hard roads and gravelly roads dulled down any excitement of the brain, and I never overtaxed it since. It is a grand thing for such as me never to wager your brain against another. As the song sang—

If you don't want to fall out of the sky
Whatever you do don't fly too high.
And said the lady to the knight—
If you don't want to fall
Don't fly at all.
And the song about
The East End Toff
Nowhere to fall but off.

The next picture I saw was a good one, it was Fred
Archer's ghost riding on a ghosted horse a race all
by themselves the two of them in the bright moonlight. The picture that hung next it was called
Maiden's Prayer; it showed a lady in a good black
velvet dress with fine well-made white hands clasped
in prayer, and her eyes were looking up. I'll say it
was painted by *some* grand artist, and I'll tell you
he meant it whoever he was, for you know there's
lots of funny tough stuff to say about the Maiden's
Prayer, but, though I saw many a hard case, in that
hall, and looking at that picture, I never heard one
of them say anything what he shouldn't. If you came
downstairs in the early morning and saw the morning
sun slanting on that girl praying away I'll tell you
it'd bring the tears into your eyes.

It brings the tears to my eyes to think of you on
those stairs looking at that picture.

That's right, sir, for you. I never was one, never
one of those plug uglies, I was always mannered, and
gentle mannered. I'd say I stood among the leatheriest
as ever drew the breath of life, and they never tried
to do me no harm. If I stood in with them I stood

183

in on my own responsibilities, and I never was no cast-iron man. Perhaps it was that I wasn't too brave, never mind why or what. I'll take off my hat to me, that was, one time, long ago.

Now, sir, old Squire, what sort of wall-picture did you see in your grand halls when you wasn't perished with your income taxes and could look a toucher in the face and not feel bound to say, "It's all the Grace of God, my boy, keeps me from acting the toucher myself, so good evening to you, take me old walking-stick and see what you can raise on it and bring me back one-half the plunder for a drink". You'd say "and it likes me well".

Ah, the pictures my juvenile eyes first saw delight in were engravings of two handsome girls—the Gunning Sisters!

What was their act? Halt, enough! I know now right enough. It comes back to me their act was something like an act. They started from scratch, I'll say, and Whiffaway where they did land! Right in front top of the ground. The bravest of them died the first. And here am I if I started from scratch it's back at scratch again now I am.

You have never asked to leave it, Madame, you always stood ready on your toes. Another picture, the next one to the Sisters, was a mighty large coloured engraving of a farmyard with uncommon glossy cows and pigs and chickens and ducks and farm horses, and a very plushy pair of sheep and a shining Milk Maid and a still more shining Farmer's Boy. And a large barn and a farmhouse in the old Christmas pantomime Manor House style. The next picture was a portrait, not very big but with very penetrating eyes, it was of an old sportsman in a green coat. He had a white muffler round his throat and his face was of a musty red tinge. The people held that it was very like and was of my grandmother's younger brother. He looked to me, to my youthful eyes—I've never seen the painting since I was in my youth, it was sold by auction when a lot of good old phizes, that's a good word, were sold—to my youthful eyes he looked to me like a man who would sing a good song. The next pictures, all these pictures as I remember them together, hung in the breakfast-room. The next picture was another large-sized coloured engraving, it was by an artist called Herring, it was of a steeplechase. There were five horses coming down a little bit of a slope to a tall stone wall, a masoned wall. There was a horse right in front, a blue-black horse, the man riding him very tall and handsome like I might have been a few years later, long stirrups, and he was letting blue-black come at that wall very fast. There was another horse, a bay, a little into the picture, coming over the wall like a bird. And farther off there was a grey rising to it, you could see it'd take him all his time but he'd get over all right. That picture used to stir up my young blood, I don't know about standing each particular hair up on my head, like the fretful Porcupine, but if I was alone in the room I'd gaze my fill at that picture. There are people now who would say no horses stretch themselves so far in a gallop. But I'll say they looked like galloping to me then, and I saw that engraving, or his fellow, in a secondhand furniture shop in this City only this afternoon and I'll say those horses seemed to me to still be galloping. And they were great animals, you could see the blood in them. This artist, this Herring, he, they'll tell you, was an imaginative painter of horses—well I wish I had his imagination. The picture, in a dark corner it was, that hung on the right of the steeplechase, was a piece of embroidery, it had gone away faded to a silver-grey colour. It wasn't a cheerful picture, but it never made me unhappy to look at it, though I had a cousin, he must have been a lot older than me, because our house was to him, it appeared, the land of Come-and-help-yourself, and when he came to that picture he always said, "That thing gives me the creeps, it gives me the shivers in the backbone". And then he'd take the whiskey bottle and he'd root out a glass and fill himself out a naggin. It was nothing, this picture, more mournful than a large tomb on the bank of a fast rolling river, in some far-away place. I knew because, as well as the shaking ash hanging over the tomb, there were palm trees. The• embroidered name on the tomb was just "Robert". I always understood he was a grand uncle who died far away. My cousin pretended to me he knew well who it was, he'd say as he sluiced down the whiskey, "Ah, Bob—Bob Down". He thought that very funny, or did he I wonder? I wonder if the little cries they used to have long ago for the purpose of making a little laugh were thought as funny by the people who gave them. I am inclined to think they just threw them out because they thought it mannerly for them to use little sayings in keeping with the character they were cast for. There seemed to be no happiness in their joking. I wonder what made them truly happy, do you know I cannot tell. Perhaps this cousin of mine was as happy as ever he was at the sight of a good morning with the sun breaking up under the clouds and driving them slowly away.

Well, now, I thought all the old ones were just as happy as they could be all the day long, that was what they told me. "Ah, how happy I was when I was a girl, singing like a bird all the day long," they'd say. Come to think of it, Squire, you are on the right lay, though you spoil my beliefs in these old ones. You make me know that I never heard one truthful statement made by any one older than myself unless they couldn't possibly help it. It's only a year or two now since I first heard a word of truth. Am I telling the truth myself? I am, it is the truth.

I think, man, you worry yourself needlessly—or do you?

No, I don't worry. I'm glad to think I lived in a mist of lies because I know now I didn't bother to believe or not believe what they told me. And I don't think they'd care themselves either, it was just a sort of habit they had of deceiving the young.

And what other pictures had you while you breakfasted?

Though it was called the Breakfast Room, I never took a breakfast there. It was a place I would go in the afternoon to look at a picture-book when I was a child, and later to think over some grievance I thought I had, perhaps nothing worse than an every-day jacket getting a bit grey at the elbows, and an objection from above to my relegating Sunday's jacket to every day, and having a new Sunday complete turn-out. Seldom worse on my mind than that, though that was bad enough. The room I ate my breakfast in, in the winter for warmth, was a sort of a pantry off the hall full of old coats and rugs with horses' hairs in them, and old walking-sticks. In the summer I took my breakfast in an especially grand situation, I was the only one in the house above the baize door who could hit the trail and breakfast together. I took my summer mornings' breakfasts in what was the largest of the two drawing-rooms. The other one was a sort of a little apologetic cave, a place that made you think of everything but comfort. In the large one where I took my breakfast in the middle of the grandeur, or, speaking truly, towards one end, on a round table they'd set it out for me. And when I sat down I'd have on my left hand a tall western window showing the light but no sunshine. But if the sun was bright my breakfast got a little share of it for there was a window high up in the eastern wall of the room. The drawing-room was up to its own roof, and that was higher than any other roof in the whole make of the house. Through that little high-up window a shaft of sunlight would come down on to my table and give me a gold platter to eat my bacon and eggs off. At my back I'd have the whole length of the stately room behind me. I'll tell you on an innocent morning I felt like an Emperor. Sufficient to the day is mortgage thereof.

Right before me, filling a third of the northern wall, was a large painting of a dell, a kind of a tinker's hollow in a classical land, a tall pillar or two standing on the right, a tall pillar lying broken down in the middle distance and in the foreground a rushing stream. I don't think it was such a very classical-looking stream. I had my own idea that the painting was a spectacular development of some travelling artist's ideas of a native park. We had a stream running through our place, and though I stood to every side of it, leaping over it this way and that, and tried to get a view over it that might have suggested the same to the artist, I never got it right. I forgot to say that there was a dancing group of young god-desses in the very centre of the dell in the painting. Perhaps if I'd seen them dancing the other side of our stream I would have agreed that the artist had painted our place, and nobody else's place.

I believe you, Squire.

Well, it was a long time ago, and if any body standing by a stream saw me at this moment capering on the grass, I'd have the heart to forgive them if they said that the days of the classical dances for all ages and shapes of the human form were a thing of the past. The picture next to the park was a very small water-colour of two very rosy apples with a bunch of primroses in front of them tied with a little piece of light-blue ribbon. I thought it a very beautiful little picture. The gilt mount on it was a little mottled but though it had a great space of empty wall on each side of it it held its chin up against everything in that end of the room. There was no name on it so I suppose now it was a copy by some amateur that I'll say was good enough to meet any one. On the eastern side of the apples there was a large painting intended to balance the classic park. It was of a ship, the *Beholder*, her name was very clear on her bow. She was sailing towards me as I sat at my breakfast, sailing to the West, I liked to think, for I hoped some day to sail to the West to a fairyland I often thought of—the United States of America. She was a full-rigged ship, three masts. A man with a life behind him the greater part of it spent as a sailor, spent is the word judging by what he told us, said it was "a perfect representation of a ship with all plain sail set close hauled on the port tack and every block on her is right. The man that painted her knew a ship". So my uncle, when he showed a visitor that picture of *Beholder*, always told them that everything about her was absolutely correct, and would repeat what the sailor said about her word for word. He got a great relief to himself and even a pleasure in knowing that on a wall there in that old house there was a representation of something without a flaw in it, without a blemish. He liked to look closely at the little curl of white water round the bows of the ship. He thought of the ship as moving always but never moving away from him. His speech about the picture as he showed it off would be the longest speech he would make to any visitor. He generally made it pretty early in the visit. While he made it the visitor would generally stand long-faced and stupidly by, and when it was over he would wait expecting to have to listen to other speeches about other pictures, and perhaps even he would point to some other picture, the classic park scene perhaps, and say, "And this one looks interesting, very valuable I am sure". But my uncle wouldn't have anything to say. Indeed the visitor would not hear from him more than three words together again. A good deal of the easterly wall of that drawing-room was taken up with a fireplace full of ferns in pots, and two looking-glasses. Over the bell-pull to one side there was an oval brown-coloured portrait of a bright and tough-looking ancestor. Eighteenth-century sportsman, good-looking, better looking than me this minute. It wasn't very large, but it was impressive looking particularly to me, because just then I was reading some old novels of eighteenth-century life in England and I had been told that the subject of this red-brown chalk drawing had fought five or six duels over in Bristol and he seemed to me to have been a hero. I had another ancestor, we didn't have a drawing of him, he was called "Curly" and after he had insulted a stranger, in a town far away, he received the stranger's glove across the bridge of his nose, and so was driven to call the man out. The stranger selected swords as the weapons of honour. Five o'clock on a summer's morning they met under the walls of the old castle in the centre of the place with smooth grass running all round it.

There was a nurse with two children, one in a trolly, the other to foot. Living in a house convenient to the field of war, she heard about the duel by chance in the Apple and Cabbage shop, and so out she went with the two children, and at twenty minutes to four she'd spread herself and the children on the top of a green slope that came up to the castle wall, all set to see the bloodshed. She saw a doctor and four very well-dressed men, seconds, two each to a man, and there was a little cake cart there, and the man who owned it had a couple of dishes piled up with sandwiches on it and some hot chocolate set on a little turf fire. And when those two duellists arrived they rode up one on a big-boned grey and the other on a bright chestnut, and they fell to admiring each other's mounts and then they fell to cheapening them. And in a minute they were side by side with the horses' heads turned the same way with the sun on their right hands, though they were in the shelter of the castle. And one sung out so that nurse could hear, indeed they talked so loud all the time she never missed a thing. He sung out, "I race you twice round for the breakfast," and the other said, "Twice is no test, six times round"—let the doctor count. "Well. Away now. Off, off now, all right off"; and they were away side by side watching each other. They went out of the nursemaid's sight. They were away a while and when they came back my old relative—his was the grey, he wasn't old then—was about a length in front and pretending to look back, so round again much the same and the grey listening with his ears back for the chestnut. The man on the chestnut the fourth time round sings out, "Doctor, tell us when it's the last round, sing out clear". When the doctor sang out "last time" my old friend was two lengths in front, but the chestnut was gathering herself for an effort. Last time round and the winning-post. I suppose the cake cart was that, for the doctor and the seconds were there. Right on the winning-post my old fellow seemed to go a bit wide, the nurse thought, and up comes the chestnut and they couldn't make anything of it, but as near a dead heat as ever that nursemaid saw. And after that they had some hot mugs of chocolate, though the jockeys were hot enough the nurse said, and "Damb the lie," she said, "but never a duel they had at all that morning or any other morning, as far as I ever heard of".

That was Curly's duel.

The other side of the fireplace there was another bell pull. A false one it was, it didn't have any attachment to any bell, though it had an old red rosette on it. That was the bell I pulled one afternoon when I had a bit of an altercation with a red-faced young cousin of mine who had too much to say for himself altogether, and most of it was about my father and he was dead. And most of it was true. So I gave the bell pull a strong pull, and I said, "See here, bright lad, I'll have my uncle's man put you out". It was a good bluff, it was good because it worked good. That young cousin of mine went out promptoh. He never looked right or left, but heel and toe, out of the drawing-room door, across the hall, out of the front door, down the steps and away with him for home. I wish every time I ever tried to pull a bluff since it had worked so well. Anyway the other side of the bell pull there was a bluey-looking drawing, a pastel tall and narrow of a young

man in a long blue riding coat, white breeches and
boots with yellow tops and his hair powdered and
tied up with black ribbon. An old lady, oh mighty
old she was at the time and it's a long time ago, said
the young man was like me when he was a boy. Old
liar! She was only boasting of her age. That's one
thing I never was tempted to do, boast of my age, I
might have swanked about my youthfulness off and
on. The next picture was another old-fashioned one,
it was of a coach-and-four, grey horses with pink
roses in their head stalls and they galloping in a
moonlight scene, and what do you think, but the
coachman wasn't a man at all but a young woman
with a wide straw hat with flowers on it, and a scarf
of silk round her neck and it blowing out behind,
and hells blast, I beg your pardon, Madame, but
not a single other human being on the top of the
coach but the young woman. Inside the coach there
was a lantern there in the roof, so the inside was
illuminated, and there was sitting, doubled up, a
battered-looking old boy with a wideawake hat tied
down with string and an account book in his hand
and he with a pencil in his old claw making up the
accounts. My uncle would show that picture to any
young woman who came to the house, and he'd
stand back and he'd puff out his chest and he'd pull
forward the locks of hair in front of his ears, and
he'd say, "Oh never marry a miser". He never had a
red cent himself, poor old lad, to be miserly with.
Over the door high up there was a picture of a
church and a churchyard and a bunch of old trees
and a great building of rooks, and that old uncle

whenever he passed out of the door before me would look up at them and say, "Those fellers'd like to be picking my old bones". But they never got a chance for he was never buried near a churchyard but on a hillside. God rest his soul! He never had fear. But there was a mort of pictures hanging on the walls in that old house. I didn't notice them except that I knew they were there and they sank into my store of memory. I never tried to recall them before, but it would be a weariness of the flesh, whatever that means, unfortunately the flesh is never weary long, to listen to me describing them.

No, no, heave ahead in this sea, the waves lick the ship's stern without jealousy as an ocean sea.

Well said, well said, same sayer again, or presently.

On the first landing I know there was a picture, an engraving of two lovers by a wall, an Italian fisherman and his lass, very choice—both of them. And near a landing window there hung a coloured engraving of a gamecock. And because whenever the window was open, or indeed when it was not, there was always the chance of a whirl of wind coming along the passage, and that wind would whirl the gamecock picture on his string and so he was always crooked, looking up defiantly or bowing in humility. I often straightened him for himself. But what were the early pictures that you, sir, yourself first saw?

They were curious enough. But we wait now for Master Bowsie's pictures, and then, Madame, let you be recalling yours for you must be next if you will. Now, Bowsie, don't beat about the bush. Up with the bucket straight out of the well. The truth, all the truthful pictures, and nothing but the truth.

I'll tell you, the first picture I ever drew my young attention to was hanging at the back of the hall door, so that it was liable to fall off when the door was opened suddenly. It was not a painting in oils or waters but an engraving out of an old illustrated paper, it was in a frame without glass, or maybe it had glass once and got it shivered falling down. It showed an old-fashioned railway engine with a tall funnel sticking up into the sky like a plug hat in the noonday, and it had a few open trucks behind it full of nasty-faced-looking guys and their ladies very simpery, and flags every way sticking out of the chest of the engine, and "God damn the lie", as the girl said, but the engineer and his second in command had on tall hats. And then there was a lot of fat-looking guys standing all over the place and on the tracks right in front of the engine. I always thought of the song:

> The Bulgine bust
> And the hoss ran off
> And he killed five thousand niggar.

I tell you every time I saw that picture, and that was every time I went out of the hall door, I remembered that song. It was a very narrow hall cluttered up with a hat and coat-stand and the stairs coming down from the top storey. And one time there'd been a little girl living in that house, the idolized daughter of an idiotic old bloke. His missus was one of those fulsome, but stately, dames who one time used to like to accentuate the curvature of their necks by wearing a man's linen collar very open at the front with curling-out points like a circus ringmaster's collar. And they produced this child and it surely was an idol. And the old father he wasn't fit to walk upstairs without some help, it's a fact, but he climbed up the step ladder and he balanced his old self on the penultimate top of the ladder and he screwed two big iron hooks into the ceiling where there was a rafter, and he had to prod a lot before he found a rafter, and the plaster all the time coming down on his old flat face. And when he got those hooks in, his wife dusted the plaster off her bust and handed up the old man the two rings of the two ropes of a swing with a yellow wooden seat. And the old lad came down, and when the little idol came back from school, very particular little school, only five other pupils, they put her sitting in the swing, and she swung herself until no grown person in the living world, except those parents, could have stuck it. They'd go in and sit in the front room and come out again and have a look at her still swinging. She was pretty well brought up on that swing for the next couple of years. I believe she must have hit that engine picture if it had been there, but of course it wasn't, it was an heirloom brought in by my family when they moved in. But the swing hooks were still up in the ceiling.

But if that little pet girl didn't get the engine picture she pretty near got the postman, so I've been told, under the chin one morning with both hooves.

Her old dad died, and after a time her mum died, and this girl, that idolized swinger, carved her name on the Roll of Fame. "Swing high, swing low!" How goes it? But this isn't pictures, except in the misty curtains of the concealéd eye. In the front room there were two pictures and two only, one was of Heenan in an attitude of self-defence, and if the picture had been of the other fellow I would have pitied Heenan. The second picture was a photograph of a fine girl playing Rosalind and she'd signed it across the lower right-hand corner and on a slant, so large and so affectionately that I never was able to make out the name. Anyway I expect she was dead before I ever saw her picture. Up on the landing at the back there was a picture, if you are willing to count something out of a frame as a picture. It was a kind of a bird's-eye view of the Crimea war and it was stuck on, pasted on, to the wall, I believe, to hide a discoloration of the wall-paper where the last tenants, the father and mother of the swinging child, had something hanging which by covering the wall-paper kept it from fading in the sunlight which was very strong up there, as strong sunlight as ever I saw in the whole of my life. On the exposed wall it'd take you all your time to make out what sort of a concern the pattern was at all. It might be horses jumping over fences innumerable, or gilded cages with canaries in them singing, or baskets of flowers wriggling in a breeze, or fairy ships on a fairy sea. But where the hanging thing, it might have been the hat of the mother of the swinging kid, hung you could make out, clear as a bush, the wallpaper it was, a series of water parties in boats with fishing-rods and every damn thing that goes with not evening dress, as Rudyard Kipling said, but with white flannel trousers, and pale blue belts with brass clasps, and striped shirts and donkeys' breakfasts with 1st Zingari ribbons on the damned uncomfortable things. You'll excuse me, miss, but you never wore a hard straw hat, or if you did you had enough of a cushion of your shining locks up top side to take up the crushing down of the awful core of the twirl of the straw where it began in a prod of hard spike that would be capable of penetrating the skull of a national school master. And that's all the pictures that entered into my soul.

Now for the lady's tableaux.

The first picture you ever saw was your own face in a looking-glass and you thought it was a lovely sight, and some silly girls told you the same and you believed them and it cost you dear. The first pictures I saw with my little eyes were Oil paintings all very fine and large:

> The largest in creation,
> They're all very fine—and large,
> The Green vales,
> The round towers,
> The mountains,
> The lakes, and the bright rivers
> Of our dear Land of Ireland.

From my dear Mammy's shawl I saw them, when she whipt me up, wrapt me up and danced down the street to the house where my bold dad did the Macrah Macree Act with all our money, throwing pints about and absorbing his share of them himself. The paintings were all along the wall. They were strong paintings for they stood up to the rolling along of every old bad actor and stevedore between the bridges and the buffling sea. I'd look out of the shawl and I'd call out clear, "Hello, dad, you're looking grand". My first part, my mother taught it to me. "Ah," my father would say, "the beauties of home life. Farewell, gentlemen, all the rest is on the house, and the house is on me"—and when we three got out in the street my Mamma would say, "Sir, I almost thought once you looked like a gentleman. How much have you left?" As mild as a shorn sheep my papa would hold up his hand with a little gathering of white pieces and brown. My Mamma would take them from him without a word and put them in my two little fat fists. I was the bank. My Mammy knew that no matter how many bright shining licensed houses we passed, my Daddy would not rob me, not if his tongue was blistering for one last go down. Those were the first pictures I ever saw and the other night I was passing by and I spit on my handkerchief and I polished the wall by the door and as I'm a living woman and no one says I'm not, there was my round tower still holding his own. I have seen many pictures since but first come first served. What about talking of something to the end of our lives so far away from the beginning. Did any of you ever think of yourselves dying and how you would like to die?

But, Madame, not yet our latter ends. Wait a while for pity's sake, let us hear what the Good Boy saw on the wall after he saw the looking-glass, and then after that we must have himself here in the duskiness. He said the pictures he saw first were curious. Now, Good Boy, what tableaux first lifted the black mantillas of your lashes?

I saw myself as others saw me in that looking-glass and I hope I'll never see myself looking that way again. A face like an apple with hair like a ship's mop. It is since those days that by artifice I moulded for myself the graceful lined cheek, the Grecian nose, the resolute chin, the noble brows—

Desist, enough.

Brows. The rippling locks hanging like cows' tails over a chalky cliff.

Hanging like vine leaves over a marble tomb. I turned from the looking-glass and my youthful eyes were gladdened with a picture of a ship in full sail just like his Honour's own, only my ship, I believe, was wrong in every detail. It was painted by a carriage builder and he was a good carriage builder; along the top of the frame lay balanced there a long whip with its lash brought back in a couple of loops and made fast to the stock. It was the last whip of a famous whip and I have forgotten his name. No, I never knew it. They said he was called Ted, but they said that wasn't his right name. The mystery of the whip. The next picture I saw would be, I believe, a tall engraving from a picture by Sir Frederick Leighton—

The Bath of Psyche.

The next picture was a large photograph of Heenan the pugilist. He was in his street clothes, not in an attitude of war the way the Baron had him, but with the assured eye. And an engraving of Tom Sayers hung there. So we were all in classic line. But the pictures I studied most of all were on the top of a small round table in our front room. It was a congregated mass of Christmas cards glued there and varnished. I used to sit in the armchair with the table on my lap so as I could work my way through all those simple pretty things, old cottages in a sunset, birds on little bushes, robins in the snow of course, but plenty other birds too. And old Christmas scenes of waits singing with a horn lantern for company. And punch bowls with jolly squires, like his Honour here, doing the honours of the bowl with great long-handled ladle to ladle it out. I knew about punch, I had a tumbler full for myself on Christmas night. I think it must have been broken down a good deal for my little noddle. And I see a picture now at this moment, and I never could have seen it fully. I see myself a lovely little boy, well made, well standing, good to look at if you forgot the plain phiz and the bunch of hair, a pinafore on me and my little steaming tumbler in my hands. I could pipe my eye a little, now this moment, when I think of my little self so sweet so long ago. And now about this—did you hear me strike my chest?—about this straight-formed but crooked-minded withered sapling of perishing humanity the least said the better. That's the finish of me. Let's have the truth, the whole truth, and nothing but the truth, from the man here who started the pictured ball a rolling.

I promised too much and now I feel full of the deaths I longed for when death was far away. I said a while ago that the first pictures I saw were curious and the word, I am sure, has a different meaning to all of us here present. Anyway to myself the first pictorial ornament hanging on a wall was a coloured woodcut of Punch and Judy, and I thought it very stupid because Punch and Madame Judy and the dog Toby and the Hangman were all with huge heads which I know now were of political personages of the day. I thought them a disgusting lot of igno-ramuses. I had seen a real Punch and Judy and I knew what they should be like. I thought Toby a wonderful actor and Punch's own voice I thought sublime. Hark, listen! is that a corncrake I hear calling to his love? Surely in St. Stephen's Green a corncrake must be a visitor from the wider spaces. Do not let us interrupt his love song.

I wish it was his love song to the dawn. I'm tired of this night, it is long, and long drawn out.

Well, let us cut it shorter with the tales of our latter ends—and, Bowsie, I mean no joke—my joking days are over. When we come down to the stones of our fancied departures, joking is obscene. Departures—making our departures. When sailors made their departures they knew and noted the points of the compass, within the circle of the com-pass card they made their farewell. Our farewells are within no circle. Lady, before you forget. How did you wish to die?

That's better. I know well what I wished my death to be. When I was a young girl I was the same height as I am now and I weighed but six stone. If you could have had an X-ray of me there was nothing to me but heart. I declare on my oath it beat so grand the very first time I played Miss FFoillett in Willy Reilly that when the boy says " I will not leave you until you are safe within your father's home, while I seek a precarious existence amidst the rocky fastness of the mountains or the gloomy caverns of the lakes," and the drummer boomed the drum with the fat of his hand, and then stopped, I did not know he'd stopped. I thought the drum was still sounding for the gloomy caverns. But it was mine own heart was booming fit to shake the woodlands down. After that I declared to myself, and I believed myself, that I would ask for no better death than to die with Reilly holding up my body. I had it all set out. I would look my last look but one on him, and give my last to the band and the people, and they'd stand up and they would give me a lament soft and low as I fell on sleep. I had nothing on my mind to forgive. I would like a little more time now to forgive. That is a death I often cried over and the Willy Reilly I had in my eye he got a quick enough death, poor dear boy, and not so long after I had arranged my death-bed, or my death-standing, to be so close to him, and I am alive. That's a queer thought. I chose my death and I was satisfied with my planning of it for many a year at that time, and now I know I will have no choice. I never chance a reading of the cards. I never ask for a tossing of the old tea leaves. When it comes God give me the strength not to be so that I am ashamed of myself. I die when I must and I hope I die game and is that a sin, Squire? A sin of vanity or pride? If it is a pride, it isn't a pride in myself for any good whatsoever to myself. It is a pride to be able to die for the honour of all the game things that do die in the hope eternal. Or if it is sure that the poor beasts have no thoughts to hope with, they can, I know, die in the eternal, and in that eternal I must die. Your friends of the dark night have taken me unawares. I never thought to talk so seriously to you. I thought I could talk all in fun of Willy Reilly and his fair Colleen Bawn. Now, now, Mister Bowsie, what death did you long for if you ever longed to die?

Is it my turn again so soon? I arranged for myself many deaths, always glorious or always at anyrate striking and sometimes embarrassing to my friends. I had grievances when I was a little boy, I thought my mother slighted me for a cousin of mine. He was so clean and bloody bright. Madame, I beg your pardon, 'tis graceless of me to use a stupid adjective before you. Anyway, I was to die run over by a large carriage and pair. We didn't have the motor-car for running over little boys when I was young, and it is very sure, Madame, you find it hard to think a young spirit like mine is capable of living in a casing of a body as old as the day before the motor. I had some idea of rushing out and saving my young cousin with my young body, and then mangled lying on a stretcher carried by six men. I chose them carefully, I chose them, as an honour, among men who I knew either to speak to or just by sight. They would all have their hats off prematurely. But my death would be certain, I would not have any pain only a pleasant weakness, I would lift one white hand and let it fall again and I would smile sadly and sweetly and my cousin would weep, I think, loudly. My mother would be splendid and I would forgive her all the neglect. I never got to the actual moment of my departure. I had not got the imagination or I was afraid to put it to the touch for fear I might be taken at my word. I worked off a lot of steam on it. But I have had lots of other endings of life arranged. If the lights here were not so dim I couldn't own to such things, even Bowsie can blush. I have died leading forlorn hopes, in every country over the world, and in every uniform, even in the five-bob grey flannel pants and the short-armed singlet, or in no uniform at all but the buff and a spear in one hand and a lariat in the other. Those that stood around me in my dreams, put there by myself, never knew how little of the forlorn there was about me. I have lived many lives and loved them all. I have died many deaths and loved them all. They say a coward dies a thousand deaths, a brave man but once. What about the man who died a thousand of them in imagination and still dies the thousand and one death—alone biting on the whip— a brave one, God give me sense anyway and bravery may follow. Now, Baron, how did you fancy yourself in dying? "What better," said the flying fox hunter, "than to die in the middle of a beautiful green field."

There's too many yoicks and tally-ho's in that dirge,
I think.

I never gave a thought on the way I'd like to be
taken away from this sour place. In my childhood
the most of my thoughts were given to getting
enough to eat to keep the narrow soul rattling
around inside me, if you'll excuse me speaking
freely. What about the gardener watchman? He
ought to have some ideas on how he'd like to die.
Him surrounded with so many beautiful flowers
and shrubs and the ducks and all and the statuary.
I'd like well to hear him telling out about the sort
of latter end he would like. Being both mouldy and
young he ought to be worth hearing on his demise.
But I suppose he's sleeping now with his head under
his wing, and isn't it a very uncommon thing that
all of us are awake, wide awake, I'd say, and I'm
none of your night birds—not any more. If we had
the gardener here now in the midst of us I wonder
what he'd say.

I know what he'd say. He'd say he'd like to die
thinking of me. Gardeners are always thinking about
girls, young or old.

Gardeners are not the only ones so afflicted.

You say your part as if you'd learnt it out of a
book.

What book?

No book. I never longed to die in my youth, nor
in my middle age, and not now until this moment
with my little old round head shaking on the top of
my withering neck. I would like to die this moment
with my good company. The lady here would give

me the good hand and the pleasant road. Mister Bowsie here would promise me a drink when the houses open if I'll promise not to die yet. The old bloke himself would give me his arm and he'd tell me I wouldn't be so bad looking at all if I had the old moustache burnt off me, and he'd tell me that in his youth he was such another as myself and that would please me. He'd talk to me as if I was a man and a brother with a nut with brains inside it not just a shell—dusty empty. Dusty roads, red roads, red sandy roads, four wheels spinning sixteen, that's right sixteen, ain't I good at arithmetic, sixteen shoes rattling on the road. I give up the memory of them all, the posthorn and the whip, in the air. You've heard songs of the Harp in the air, I would give and I tell you, and it is true, I would give them all up to die quietly here by this seat in the shadow of this tree, with all your smiling mouths kind to me and your smiling eyes to smile into mine, and mine shadowed over. And you can bury my body where 'tis most convenient. Some are all for burials. A four-horse hearse is a nice thing. Well, here's four-horse hearses to you all.

You're too soon, Sir.

He is right, should the fair one smile one should die. Because when she smiles, she is absorbed in her smile thinking what a nice smile it is, and so she's not worrying about you, and you can make your getaway. "It would have been money in my pocket," man said, if when Eve smiled the first time Adam had cleared out.

You speak in puzzles.

I've heard a boy, not such a good boy, say that the tree of the knowledge of good and evil was a monkey-puzzle tree.

Fie for shame!

I said so. I am not able to bear the remembrance of most of the deaths I fancied myself dying. Many of them are too trivial to mention. What a trifling death it seems now the one I wished for about—well, fifteen years ago. My neck broken on the landing side of the largest fence of them all, my head in the lap of the beautiful nurse nearly as good-looking as yourself, mam, and with white long hands. She would be just lifting back the curls from my brow, and all the time, at two-minute intervals, she would be saying, "Do not worry". Why should I? It'd only just be a manner of speech and all the time weaving and marching round me, me in the centre of them, as the radius would be, all the flat-faced bookmakers and others I owed my money to in this earthly shade, and they'd be singing all low and together.

Death wipes the platter clean.

And Nursie saying, "Do not worry". But I would not give two penn'orth of gin for a death like that now. I would want something more stylish. Remember I don't want anything quaint, I don't want any special costume business, no old men's club singing old catches, no, not even a cinema organ. One time I would have liked, I was in that mood at the time, to die among a lot of horses and they out at grass, just cropping their food round me, and me lying there still and silent. For a man who talked his share, I always have a place, a pocket in my heart, for silence.

The horses would move quietly round me and they would never stand on me. But I wouldn't like to fall down to die in the middle of horses stampeding, or, worse still, men stampeding, trampling, trampling. It's easier to imagine the death you wished away from yourself than the one you wished to you. But there is a place for my death which I always have pictured in the back of my imagination. It is on a terrace I am, old-fashioned, white terrace, high above trees, and a river coming from the west and winding, and flat grass on the south bank, and people, men and women, young and tall, walking on it looking towards their shadows as they walk along them towards me, and under me. The woods are green, and full, on either bank, and though I know there are houses among the trees, I see the place as it was long ago and the tree lands and the grassy hills run away and away to the far sea by common-lands and furzy downs, chasing away always to the blue hills until they become the blue hills of the ocean sea. And by me on the broad balustrade of the terrace I have my long tumbler. "Hemlock", they said. No, "Lethe", they said. No pain. If I drink of it only in a dream. I know I dream of what I will never drink. Come hog, dog, or devil, lady, I know you know, I will die with my fists in front. I may turn a bit here to this side or to that, but you know I will face the hard spriggy white man of death not as you would wish me to, but as you cannot help yourself wanting me to. Come now all dead but two—the old blade and his nibs standing here behind me.

Well, here goes. I never faced death even in fancy, I hadn't got the heart for it. I never was able to contemplate its approach in others but with anguish. A child of earth, perhaps death itself, the funeral dragging along the country road, or hobbling over the paving stones, I could stand. I could even take a sort of enjoyment in it and buy myself and my most talking friend a few glasses of the hard stuff, the paraphernalia of funerals always included the hard stuff. When I must face my own death I hope to be able to remember some cheerful expression for the watchers, and how many will they be at my bedside? I've let you all down now in life for I have no death story to tell. But hurry, hurry, with the last of the braves, or one fair and four braves. But the fair is a brave one in my way of thinking too. Come now, M.C., Referee, Bottle Holder, Conscience Handler, Time-keeper, Judge and Starter, the early pictures of your walls were to be curious, your eyes of death should be uproarious.

Old Bos, you have said my imagining of death should have been uproarious. I planned many such endings dramatic in the spotlight, or alone, with myself my only audience, myself holding the candle to myself. I suppose in my cradle I swung a rattle and enjoyed the sound of it, and alone, I suppose, I could have appreciated the death-rattle in my throat. My old friend heard his own and lived forty years to drink to the memory of that rattle on forty birthdays. I have to reject all those fancy passings for one passing word from you all. But as we move and huddle about here, a universality, a darkness, is passing.

Look over your left shoulder, old blade, and is that not the peep of day away through the trees and in that slip among the houses?

It is the dawn of day, the Peep of Day, boys.

Maybe it's just the false dawn.

No, the dawn comes slicing in, though some of you can't see it. I see the reflection of it.

It is the false dawn.

No, I saw that a while ago.

Come, let us get away, if we can now, we are all ready to go.

I saw a ladder under a tree up this alley-way of trees.

That's the talk. Up with it against the railings. I heard the Cop's feet receding along toward the east a while ago.

Now, lady, up the ladder and we'll hand you down. I will hand you down to the Baron here who will go over first to catch. Come, we beseech you.

No, let me wait a while. I turn back again into the shade, and here I lean myself against the stone base of this statue, and I don't know, rock, what statue it is you support, but you are cool, and in coolness we pray best. So I pray, dear Lord, you do but bless all these poor men and bless the poor soul—the gardener. Hold the ladder for me now—I am coming. I know, and it's not far from the Daisy Market, and there's a man awake there, and he is making coffee in a place there—I know it well. I'll find it myself so the blessing of God is on us all, and on all your ways and my ways—and so farewell, farewell, farewell, farewell.

Farewell to you also.

215

216

220

225

229

231

234